Sharing a room with Isla McKenna.

It was the sensible solution, Harry knew. The problem was, he didn't *feel* sensible. He was already on edge about the wedding, and if they shared a bed it would be all too easy to seek comfort in her.

She's your colleague, he reminded himself. Off limits. She wants a relationship just as little as you do. Keep your distance.

He'd just about got himself under control by the time he'd changed into the tailcoat, wing-collared shirt and cravat his father had asked him to wear. He left the top hat on the bed for the time being, took a deep breath and knocked on the bathroom door.

'Isla, I'm ready whenever you are,' he said, 'but don't take that as me rushing you. There's plenty of time. I just didn't want you to feel that you had to be stuck in there while I was faffing about in the other room.'

She opened the door. 'I'm ready,' she said softly.

Harry had never seen Isla dressed up before. He'd seen her wearing jeans and a T-shirt, and he'd seen her in her uniform at the hospital. On every occasion she'd worn her hair pinned back and no make-up, not even a touch of lipstick.

Today she was wearing a simple blue dress that emphasised the colour of her eyes, a touch of mascara, the lightest shimmer of lipstick—and she looked stunning. Desire rushed through him, taking his breath away. How had he ever thought that Isla would be *safe*? He needed to get himself under control. Now.

Dear Reader,

Her Playboy's Proposal is all about trust—learning to trust again when someone's let you down, and learning to trust yourself when you think you're the one who's let everyone down.

And how do you learn to trust? In Harry and Isla's case, they discover that love is the answer. Except they take a while to realise it—and it takes a life-changing moment to make them both realise that they can trust each other *and* themselves.

The story's set partly in Cornwall (if you're thinking *Poldark*—absolutely!), partly in London and partly on the coast in Dorset. And there are weddings, best men, best women and a speech I really, *really* enjoyed writing.

I hope you enjoy Harry and Isla's journey.

I'm always delighted to hear from readers, so do come and visit me at www.katehardy.com.

With love,

Kate Hardy

HER PLAYBOY'S PROPOSAL

BY
KATE HARDY

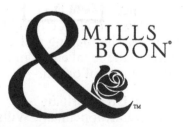

First published in Great Britain 2016
By Mills & Boon, an imprint of HarperCollins*Publishers*
1 London Bridge Street, London, SE1 9GF

Large Print edition 2016

© 2016 Pamela Brooks

ISBN: 978-0-263-26106-6

Our policy is to use papers that are natural, renewable
and recyclable products and made from wood grown
in sustainable forests. The logging and manufacturing
processes conform to the legal environmental
regulations of the country of origin.

Printed and bound in Great Britain
by CPI Antony Rowe, Chippenham, Wiltshire

Kate Hardy has always loved books, and could read before she went to school. She discovered Mills & Boon books when she was twelve, and decided that this was what she wanted to do. When she isn't writing Kate enjoys reading, cinema, ballroom dancing and the gym. You can contact her via her website: www.katehardy.com.

To my fellow Medical authors—
because you're a really lovely bunch
and I'm proud to be one of you. xxx

CHAPTER ONE

ISLA TOOK A deep breath outside the staffroom door. Today was her second day at the emergency department of the London Victoria Hospital, and she was still finding her place in the team. She'd liked the colleagues she'd met yesterday, and hopefully today would go just as well—with new people who didn't know her past and wouldn't judge her. She pushed the door open, then smiled at the nurse who was checking the roster on the pinboard. 'Morning, Lorraine.'

'Morning, Isla. You're on cubicles with Josie and Harry the Heartbreaker this morning,' Lorraine said.

'Harry the Heartbreaker?' Isla asked.

Lorraine wrinkled her nose. 'I guess that's a bit of a mean nickname—Harry's a good doctor and he's great with patients. He listens to them and gives them a chance to talk.'

'So he's very charming, but he's a bit careless with women?' Isla knew the type. Only too well.

'Harry dates a lot,' Lorraine said. 'He doesn't lead his girlfriends on, exactly, but hardly anyone makes it past a third date with him.'

And lots of women saw him as a challenge and tried to be the exception to his rule, Isla guessed. 'Uh-huh,' she said. She certainly wouldn't be one of them. After what had happened with Stewart, she had no intention of dating anyone ever again. She was better off on her own.

'OK, so he'd be a nightmare to date,' Lorraine said with a wry smile, 'but he's a good colleague. I'm sure you'll get on well with him.'

So professionally their relationship would be just fine; but it would be safer to keep Harry the Heartbreaker at a distance on a personal level. Isla appreciated the heads-up. 'Everyone else in the department has been lovely so far,' she said, smiling back. 'I'm sure it will be fine.'

Though she hadn't been prepared for quite how gorgeous Harry the Heartbreaker was when she actually saw him. The expression 'tall, dark and handsome' didn't even begin to do him justice.

He would've been perfectly cast as one of the brooding heroes of a television costume drama, with dark curly hair that was a little too long and flopped over his forehead, dark eyes, a strong jaw and the most sensual mouth she'd ever seen. On horseback, wearing a white shirt, breeches and tailcoat, he'd be irresistible.

Harry the Heart-throb.

Harry the *Heartbreaker*, she reminded herself.

Luckily Josie had already triaged the first patient and was ready to assist Harry, which meant that Isla had enough time to compose herself and see the next patient on the list.

Harry was a colleague and that was all. Isla had no intention of getting involved with anyone again, no matter how gorgeous the man looked. Stewart had destroyed her trust completely, and that wasn't something she'd be able to put behind her easily.

Harry finished writing up his notes and walked into the corridor to call the next patient through. He knew that Josie had gone to triage her next patient, so he'd be working with the newest member of the team, Isla McKenna. He'd been on leave yesterday when she'd started at the London Victoria and knew nothing about her, other than that she was a senior nurse.

He eyed the nurse in the corridor with interest. Even without the double giveaways of her name and her accent, he would've guessed that Isla McKenna was a Scot. She had that fine porcelain skin, a dusting of freckles across her nose, sharp blue eyes and, beneath her white nurse's cap, dark red hair that he'd just bet looked amazing in the sunlight. Pure Celt. It was a long time since he'd found someone so instantly attractive. Not that he was going to act on it. For all he knew, she could already be involved with someone; the lack of a ring on her left hand meant nothing. 'Isla McKenna, I presume?' he asked.

She nodded.

'Harry Gardiner. Nice to meet you. How are you settling in to the ward?' he asked as they walked down to the cubicles together.

'Fine, thanks. The team seems very nice.'

'They're a good bunch,' he said. 'So where were you before you moved here?'

'Scotland,' she said, her face suddenly shuttering.

Clearly she thought he was prying and she'd given him as vague an answer as she could without being openly rude. 'Uh-huh,' he said, lightly. 'Just making polite conversation—as you would with any new colleague.'

She blushed, and her skin clashed spectacularly with her hair. 'Sorry. I didn't mean to be rude,' she muttered.

'Then let's pretend we've never spoken and start again.' He held out his hand. 'Harry Gardiner, special reg. Nice to meet you, and welcome to the London Victoria.'

'Isla McKenna, sister. Thank you, and nice to meet you, too,' she said.

Her handshake was firm, and Harry was surprised to discover that his skin actually tingled where it touched hers.

Not good.

He normally tried not to date colleagues within his own department. It made things less complicated if his date turned out to have greater expectations than he wanted to fulfil—which they usually did. And instant attraction to the newest member of their team definitely wasn't a good idea.

'So who's next?' he asked. Hopefully focussing on work would get his common sense back to where it should be—firmly in control of his libido.

'Arthur Kemp, aged seventy-three, suspected stroke,' Isla said, filling him in. 'The paramedics did a FAST assessment—' the Face Arm Speech Test was used in cases of suspected stroke to check whether the patient's face seemed to fall on one side or if they could smile, whether they could hold both arms above their head, or if their speech was slurred '—and they gave him some aspirin on the way here. I've done an initial assessment.'

'ROSIER?' Harry asked. Recognition of Stroke in the Emergency Room was a standard protocol.

She nodded. 'His score pretty much confirms it's a stroke. I checked ABCD2 as well, and the good news is that his score is nil on the D—he's not diabetic. His blood sugar is fine.'

Harry picked up immediately what she was telling him—there was only one section of the test with a nil score. 'So the rest of it's a full house?'

'I'm afraid so,' she said. 'He's over sixty, he has high blood pressure and residual weakness on his left side, and the incident happened over an hour ago now.'

'Which puts him at higher risk of having a second stroke in the next two days,' Harry said. 'OK. Does he live on his own, or is he in any kind of residential care?'

'He has a flat where there's a warden on duty three days a week, and a care team comes in three times a day to sort out his meals and medication,' Isla told him. 'They're the ones who called the ambulance for him this morning.'

'So if he did have a second stroke and the warden wasn't on dut or it happened between the care team's visits, ne chances are he wouldn't be found for a few hours, or maybe not even overnight.' Harry wrinkled his nose. 'I'm really not happy with that. I think we need to admit him to the acute unit for the next couple of days, so we can keep an eye on him.'

'I agree with you. His speech is a little bit

slurred and I'm not happy about his ability to swallow,' Isla added. 'He said he was thirsty and I gave him a couple of sips of water, but I'd recommend putting him on a drip to prevent dehydration, and keep him nil by mouth for the next two or three hours. Nobody's going to be able to sit with him while he drinks and then for a few minutes afterwards to make sure he's OK—there just won't be the time.'

'Good points, and noted.'

Mr Kemp was sitting on a bed, waiting to be seen.

Isla introduced him quickly. 'Mr Kemp, this is Dr Gardiner.'

'Everyone calls me Harry,' Harry said with a smile. 'So can you tell me about what happened this morning, Mr Kemp?'

'I had a bit of a headache, then I tripped and fell and I couldn't get up again,' Mr Kemp said. 'My carer found me when she came in to give me my tablet and my breakfast.'

Isla noticed that Harry sat on the chair and held the old man's hand, encouraging him to talk. He was kind and waited for an answer, rather than rushing the patient or pressuring him to stop rambling and hurry up. Lorraine had been spot on about his skills as a doctor, she thought. 'Can you remember, either before or after you fell, did you black out at all?' Harry asked. 'Or did you hit your head?'

Arthur looked confused. 'I'm not sure. I don't think I blacked out and I don't remember hitting my head. It's hard to say.' He grimaced. 'Sorry, Doctor. I'm not much use. My daughter's husband says I'm an old fool.'

So there were family tensions, too. The chances were, if they suggested that he went to stay with his family for a few days, the answer would be no—even if they had the room to let the old man stay. 'Don't worry, it's fine,' Harry reassured him. 'I'm just going to do a couple of checks now to see how you're doing. Is that OK?'

'Yes, Doctor. And I'm sorry I'm such a nuisance.'

Either the old man was used to being made to feel as if he was a problem, or he was habitually anxious. Or maybe a bit of both, Harry thought. He checked Mr Kemp's visual fields and encouraged him to raise his arms; the residual weakness on Mr Kemp's left side that Isla had mentioned early was very clear. And there was a walking frame next to the bed, he noticed. 'Do you normally walk with a frame?'

'Yes, though I hate the wretched thing.' Arthur grimaced. 'It always trips me up. It did that this morning. That's why I fell. Useless thing.'

Harry guessed that Mr Kemp did what a lot of elderly people did with a walking frame—he lifted it and carried it a couple of centimetres above the ground, rather than leaving the feet on the floor and pushing it along and letting it support him. Maybe he could arrange some support to help the old man use the frame properly, so it helped him rather than hindered him.

'Can you see if you can walk a little bit with me?' he asked.

He helped Mr Kemp to his feet, then walked into the corridor with him, encouraged him to turn round and then walk back to the cubicle. Harry noticed that his patient was shuffling. He was also leaning slightly to the left—the same as when he was sitting up—and leaning back slightly when he walked. Harry would need to put that on Mr Kemp's notes to be passed on to any carers, so they could help guide him with a hand resting just behind his back, and stop him as soon as he started shuffling and encourage him to take bigger steps.

Once Mr Kemp was seated safely again, Harry said, 'I'm going to send you for an MRI scan, because you had a headache and I want to rule out anything nasty, but I think Sister McKenna here is right and you've had a small stroke.'

'A stroke?' Arthur looked as if he couldn't quite take it in. 'How could I have had a stroke?'

'The most likely cause is a blood clot that stopped the blood supply to your brain for a little while,' Harry explained. 'It should be cleared by now because you're able to walk and talk and move your arms, but I'm going to admit you to the acute medical unit so we can keep an eye on you for a day or two.' He decided not to tell Mr Kemp that his risk of a second stroke was higher over the next day or two; there was no point in worrying the poor man sick. Though his family would definitely need to know. 'Has anyone been in touch with your family?'

'Sharon, my carer—she should have rung my daughter, but Becky'll be at work and won't be able to come right away.' He grimaced. 'I feel bad about taking her away from her job. Her work is so important.'

'And I bet she'll think her dad is just as important as her job,' Isla said reassuringly.

'Too right,' Harry said. Even though he didn't quite feel that about his own father. Then again, Bertie Gardiner was more than capable of looking after himself—that, or his wife-to-be Trixie, who was a couple of years younger than Harry, could look out for him.

He shook himself. Not now. He wasn't going to think about the upcoming wedding. Or the fact that his father was still trying to talk him into being his best man, and Harry had done that job twice already—did he really need to do it all over again for his father's *seventh* wedding? 'We'll have had your scan done by the time your daughter comes to see you,' Harry said, 'and we'll be able to give her a better idea of your treatment plan.'

'Treatment?' Mr Kemp asked.

'The stroke has affected your left side, so you'll need a little bit of help from a physiotherapist to get you back to how you were before the stroke,' Harry said. 'I'm also going to write you up for some medication which you can take after your scan.'

'Is there anything you'd like to ask us?' Isla asked.

'Well, I'd really like a nice cup of tea,' Mr Kemp said wistfully. 'If it wouldn't be too much trouble.'

'We can sort that out in a few minutes, after you've had your scan,' Isla said. 'At the moment you're finding it hard to swallow and I don't want you to choke or burn yourself on a hot drink, but we'll try again in half an hour and you might be able to swallow better by then. And I'll make sure you get your cup of tea, even if I have to make it myself.'

'Seconded,' Harry said, 'though I'll admit my tea isn't the best and you'd be better off with coffee if I'm the one who ends up making it.' He smiled at the old man. 'We'll get things sorted out and make sure your daughter finds you.' He shook the old man's hand and stood up. 'Try not to worry. We'll make sure you get looked after properly.'

'I'll be back with you in a second, Mr Kemp,' Isla said, and followed Harry out of the cubicles.

'Can you organise a scan and then transfer him to the acute unit?' he asked quietly when they were outside the cubicle.

She smiled at him. 'Sure, no problem.'

Her smile transformed her face completely. Harry felt the lick of desire deep inside his gut and had to remind himself that his new colleague might be gorgeous, but she was also off limits. 'Thanks,' he said. 'I'll write everything up.'

It was a busy morning, with the usual falls and sprains and strains, and a six-month-old baby with a temperature that wouldn't go down and had then started having a fit. The baby's mother had panicked and asked a neighbour to drive them in rather than waiting for an ambulance, and the triage team had rushed her straight into the department.

The baby's jaws were clenched firmly together, so Harry looked at Isla and said quietly, 'Nasopharyngeal, I think.'

Almost as soon as he'd finished talking, she had an appropriately sized tube in her hand and was lubricating the end. Between them, they secured the baby's airway and gave her oxygen, and Isla was already drawing up a phial of diazepam.

Clearly she'd come across convulsions in babies before.

Between them, they checked the baby's blood glucose and temperature.

'Pyrexia,' Harry said softly. 'I'm pretty sure this is a febrile convulsion.'

'So we need to cool her down and check for infection,' Isla said. At his nod, Isla deftly took off the baby's sleep-suit and sponged her skin with tepid water while Harry checked with the baby's distraught mother when she'd last given the baby liquid paracetamol. Once the fit had stopped and the baby's temperature spike had cooled, Isla prepared everything for an infection screen.

'I've never seen anything like that before. Is Erin going to be all right?' the baby's mother asked.

'She's in the best place and you did the right thing to bring her in,' Harry reassured her. 'I think the fit was caused by her high temperature, but we need to find out what's causing that—if it's a virus or a bacterial infection—and then we can treat her properly.'

'Will she have any more fits?' Erin's mother asked.

'Very possibly,' Isla said, 'but that doesn't mean that she'll develop epilepsy. Having a high temperature is the most common cause of fits in children between Erin's age and school age. We see this sort of thing a lot, so try not to worry.'

Worry, Harry thought. Parents always worried themselves sick over small children. And so did their older siblings—especially when they were supposed to be taking care of them and things went badly wrong.

He pushed the thought away. It was years ago, now, and he was older and wiser. Plus nowadays Tasha would give him very short shrift if he fussed over her too much; she was fiercely in-dependent. And you couldn't change the past; all you could do was learn from it. Harry had most definitely learned. He never, ever wanted to be responsible for a child in that way again.

'I'm going to admit her,' Harry said, 'purely be-cause she's so young and it's the first time she's had a fit. Plus I want to find out what's causing the infection. We'll keep an eye on her in case she has more convulsions. But you can stay with her.'

'I'll take you both up to the ward and introduce you to the team,' Isla said.

'And she's going to be all right?' the baby's mother asked again.

'Yes,' Harry said, and patted her arm. 'I know it's scary, but try not to worry.'

Ha. And what a hypocrite he was. He knew that panicky feeling all too well. *Would the baby be all right?* The overwhelming relief when you knew that the baby would survive. And then the guilt later on when you discovered that, actually, there was a problem after all... Harry's mistake had come back to haunt him big time.

'Is there anyone we can call for you?' Isla asked.

'My mum.' Erin's mother dragged in a breath. 'My husband's working away.'

'OK. As soon as Erin's settled on the ward, we'll get in touch with your mum,' Isla promised.

Harry worked with Isla on most of his list of patients that morning, and he liked the fact that his new colleague was incredibly calm, had a sharp eye, and her quiet and gentle manner stopped patients or their parents panicking. The perfect emergency nurse. He had no idea where she'd trained or where she'd worked before—Scotland was a pretty big area—but he'd just bet that she was sorely missed. She'd certainly be appreciated at the London Victoria.

They hadn't had time for a coffee break all morning and Harry was thirsty and ravenous by the time he took his lunch break—late, and he knew he'd end up grabbing something fast in the canteen so he could be back on the ward in time. When he walked into the staffroom, Isla was there.

'Hi, there. Do you want to come and grab some lunch with me?' he asked.

She gave him a cool smile. 'Thanks, but I don't think so.'

He frowned. 'Why not?'

Her expression said quite clearly, *do you really have to ask?* But she was polite as she said, 'It's nice of you to ask me, but I don't think we're each other's type.'

He blinked, not quite following. 'What?'

She looked uncomfortable. 'I, um, might be new here, but that doesn't make me an instant addition to a little black book.'

Then the penny dropped. She thought he was asking her out? Some of the other staff teased him about being a heartbreaker and a serial dater, but that was far from true. He always made sure that whoever he dated knew it was for fun, not for ever. And he hadn't been asking her out on a date anyway. Obviously someone had been gossiping about him and she'd listened to the tittle-tattle rather than waiting to see for herself. 'Actually,' he said quietly, 'as you're new to the team, I was guessing that you hadn't had time to find your way around the hospital that well yet and you might not have anyone to sit with at lunchtime, that's all.'

Her face flamed, clashing with that spectacular hair. 'I—um—sorry. I'd just heard…' She broke off. 'Sorry. I'm putting my foot in it even more.'

'Heard what?' The words were out before he could stop them.

'You have, um, a bit of a reputation for, um, dating a lot.'

He sighed. 'Honestly, where the hospital grapevine's concerned, you can't win. If you don't date, then either you're gay or you've got some tragic past; and if you do date but make it clear you're not looking for a serious relationship, then you're at the mercy of everyone who wants to be the exception to the rule and you get called a heartbreaker. Not everyone's desperate to pair off and settle down.'

'I know.' She bit her lip. 'Sorry.'

But he noticed that she still hadn't accepted his invitation to join him for lunch. Which stung. Was his reputation really that bad?

Pushing down his exasperation at the hospital grapevine, Harry gave Isla his sweetest smile.

'OK, but I give you fair warning—if you try and eat a sandwich in here, you'll be lucky to finish half of it before someone calls you to help out with something.'

'I guess it's all part of working in a hospital environment,' she said lightly.

OK. He could take a hint. 'See you later,' he said.

In the canteen, Harry saw a crowd he recognised from the maternity ward and joined them. But all the while he was thinking about Isla. Why had their new nurse been so guarded? Was it just because of whatever nonsense she'd heard about him on the hospital grapevine? Or was she like that with everyone?

Just as Harry had predicted, Isla was halfway through her sandwich when someone came into the rest room and asked her to help out.

She didn't mind—it was all part and parcel of being part of a team on the busiest department in the hospital.

But she did feel bad about the way she'd reacted to Harry the Heartbreaker. Especially after he'd explained why he'd asked her to lunch; it was just what she would've done herself if a new team member had joined the practice where she'd worked on the island. She'd been unfair to him. And, even though she'd apologised, she'd felt too awkward to join him and ended up making things worse. He probably thought she was standoffish and rude. But how could she explain without telling him about the past she was trying to put well and truly behind her?

It didn't help that she found him so attractive.

Common sense told Isla that she needed to keep her distance. Apart from the fact that she'd seen a few working relationships turn really awkward and sour after the personal relationship had ended, she wasn't in the market for a relationship anyway. Particularly with someone who had the reputation of being a charmer.

Professional only, she reminded herself. She'd apologise again for the sake for their working relationship. And that would be that.

Isla was rostered on cubicles again with Josie and Harry in the afternoon. Harry had just finished with a patient who'd been brought in with a de-gloving injury; when he came out of the cubicle, she asked quietly, 'Can we have a quick word?'

'Sure.'

Isla took a deep breath. 'I wanted to apologise about earlier.'

He looked blank. 'About what?'

'I was rude and standoffish when you asked me to go to lunch with you.'

His eyes crinkled at the corners. 'Oh, that. Don't worry about it. Blame it on the hospital grapevine blowing everything out of proportion.'

She felt the betraying colour seep into her face. This would be the easy option because there was some truth in it, but he'd been kind and he didn't deserve it. 'Should've known better because hospital gossip likes to embroider things,' she said. Not just hospitals: any small community. Like an island off the coast of Scotland where everybody knew practically everything about everyone. And she of all people knew how it felt to be gossiped about unfairly. 'I was rude. And I apologise. And maybe I can buy you a cup of tea later to make up for being so horrible.'

'You weren't horrible, just a bit…well, offish. Apology and offer of tea accepted. We can have Mr Kemp as our chaperone, if you like,' he suggested.

How could he be so good-natured about it? It made her feel even more guilty. 'I guess it's a good excuse to see how he's getting on.'

'Great. It's a non-date,' Harry said.

And oh, that smile. It could light up a room. He really was gorgeous. And nice with it. And he had a sense of humour.

It would be all too easy to let Harry Gardiner tempt her.

But this nurse wasn't for tempting.

They spent their afternoon break in the Acute Medical Unit with Mr Kemp.

'Thank you for the tea,' he said.

'Our pleasure,' Isla told him with a smile.

'You won't get into trouble for being here, will you?' he checked.

This time, Harry smiled. 'It's our afternoon break. We're allowed to take it outside our own ward if we want to.'

'I'm such a trouble to you,' Mr Kemp said.

'It's fine,' Isla reassured him. 'Has your daughter been able to visit, yet?'

'She's coming straight after work. I do feel bad about it. She's had to get someone to pick up the kids.'

'All the working mums I know are great at juggling,' Harry said. 'I bet you she's picked up her friend's children before now. It won't be a problem. Everyone mucks in to help their friends. How are you feeling?'

'Well enough to go home,' Mr Kemp said. 'If I was home, I wouldn't be a burden to everyone.'

He was able to swallow again, Isla thought, but he definitely wasn't quite ready to go home. And he'd be far more of a worry to his family if he was on his own in his flat. 'I'm sure the team here will sort things out for you,' she said brightly.

And she discovered that Lorraine had been absolutely on the ball about Harry being great with patients, because he somehow managed to find out that Mr Kemp loved dogs and got him chatting about that, distracting him from his worries about being a burden.

'You were brilliant with Mr Kemp,' she said on their way back to the Emergency Department.

Harry gave a dismissive wave of his hand. 'Just chatting. And I noticed you were watching him drinking and assessing him.'

She nodded. 'I'm happier with his swallowing, but I think he'll be in for a couple more days yet. They'll want to assess him for a water infection or a chest infection, in case that contributed to the fall as well as the stroke. And they'll need to get social services in to look at his care plan as well as talk to his family. I'm guessing that he's not so good with accepting help, and from what he said to us earlier it sounded as if his son-in-law doesn't have much patience.'

'Very true.' Harry gave her a sidelong look. 'Though I know a few people caught between caring for their kids and caring for their elderly parents. It can be hard to juggle, and—well, not all parents are easy.'

'And some are brilliant.' Isla's own parents had been wonderful—they'd never believed Andrew's accusations right from the start, and they'd encouraged her to retrain in Glasgow and then move to London and start again.

'Yes, some are brilliant.' Harry was looking curiously at her.

'It takes all sorts to make a world,' she said brightly. Why on earth hadn't she moved him away from the subject of parents? Why had she had to open her mouth? 'And we have patients to see.'

'Yes, we do. Well, Sister McKenna.' He opened the door for her. 'Shall we?'

CHAPTER TWO

'Is ISLA NOT coming tonight?' Harry asked Lorraine at the bowling alley, keeping his tone casual.

'No.'

Lorraine wasn't forthcoming with a reason and Harry knew better than to ask, because it would be the quickest way to fuel gossip. Not that Lorraine was one to promote the hospital rumour mill, but she might let slip to Isla that she thought Harry might be interested in her, and that would make things awkward between them at work. She'd already got the wrong idea about him.

All the same, this was the third team night out in a fortnight that Isla had missed. On the ward, she was an excellent colleague; she was good with patients and relatives, quick to offer sensible suggestions to clinical problems, and she got on well with everyone. The fact that she didn't come to any of the team nights out seemed odd, especially as she was new to the department and going out with the team would be a good chance for her to get to know her colleagues better.

Maybe Isla was a single parent or caring for an elderly relative, and it was difficult for her to arrange someone to sit with her child or whoever in the evenings. But he could hardly ask her about it without it seeming as if he was prying.

And he wasn't; though he was intrigued by her. Then again, if it turned out that she was a single parent, that'd be a deal-breaker for him. He really didn't want to be back in the position of having parental type responsibilities for a child. OK, so lightning rarely struck twice—but he didn't want to take the risk.

'Shame,' he said lightly, and switched the conversation round to who was going to be in which team.

Two days later, it was one of the worst days in the department Harry had had in months. He, Isla and Josie were in Resus together, trying to save a motorcyclist who'd been involved in a head-on crash—but the man's injuries were just too severe. Just when Harry had thought they were getting somewhere and the outcome might be bearable after all, the man had arrested and they just hadn't been able to get him back.

'I'm calling it,' Harry said when his last attempt with the defibrillator produced no change. 'It's been twenty minutes now. He's not responding. Is everyone agreed that we should stop?'

Isla and Josie both looked miserable, but voiced their agreement.

'OK. Time of death, one fifty-three,' he said softly, and pulled the sheet up to cover their patient's face. 'Thank you, team. You all worked really well.'

But it hadn't been enough, and they all knew it.

'OK. Once we've moved him out of Resus and cleaned him up, I'll go and find out if Reception managed to get hold of a next of kin and if anyone's here,' he said.

'If they have, I'll come with you, if you like,' Isla offered.

'Thank you.' He hated breaking bad news. Having someone there would make it a little easier.

And maybe she'd know what to say when he ran out of words.

The motorcyclist, Jonathan Pryor, was only twenty-seven, and his next of kin were his parents. The receptionist had already sent a message to Resus that Jonathan's mum was waiting in the relatives' room.

'I hate this bit so much,' he said softly as he and Isla walked towards the relatives' room.

'We did everything we possibly could,' she reminded him.

'I know.' It didn't make him feel any better. But the sympathy in her blue, blue eyes made his heart feel just a fraction less empty.

Mrs Pryor looked up hopefully as they knocked on the door and walked in. 'Jonathan? He's all right? He's out of Theatre or whatever and I can go and see him?'

Harry could see the very second that she realised the horrible truth—that her son was very far from being all right—and her face crumpled.

'I'm so sorry, Mrs Pryor,' he said softly, taking her hand. 'We did everything we could to save him, but he arrested on the table—he had a heart attack, and we just couldn't get him back.'

Sobs racked her body. 'I always hated him riding that wretched motorcycle. I worried myself sick every time he went out on it because I *knew* that something like this would happen. I can't bear it.' Her voice was a wail of distress. 'And now I'll never see him again. My boy. My little boy.'

Harry knew there was nothing he could do or say to make this better. He just sat down next to Mrs Pryor and kept holding her hand, letting her talk about her son.

Isla went to the vending machine. Harry knew without having to ask that she was making a cup of hot, sweet tea for Mrs Pryor. He could've done with one himself, but he wasn't going to be that selfish. The only thing he could do now for his patient was to comfort his grieving mother.

'Thank you, but I don't want it,' Mrs Pryor said when Isla offered her the paper cup. 'It won't bring my son back.'

'I know,' Isla said gently, 'but you've just had

a horrible shock and this will help. Just a little bit, but it will help.'

Mrs Pryor looked as if she didn't believe the nurse, but she took the paper cup and sipped from it.

'Is there anyone we can call for you?' Harry asked.

'My—my husband.' She shook her head blankly. 'Oh, God. How am I going to tell him?'

'I can do that for you,' Harry said gently. 'It might be easier on both of you if I tell him.' Even though he hated breaking bad news.

Mrs Pryor dragged in a breath. 'All right— thank you.'

'And you can come and see Jonathan whenever you feel ready,' Isla said. 'I'll come with you, and you can spend some time alone with him, too. I can call the hospital chaplain to come and see you, if you'd like me to.'

Mrs Pryor shook her head. 'I've never been the religious type. Talking to the chaplain's not going to help. It's not going to bring Jonathan back, is it?''

'I understand,' Isla said, 'but if you change your

mind just tell me. Anything we can do to help, we will.'

'He was only twenty-seven. That's way too young to die.' Mrs Pryor shut her eyes very tightly. 'And that's a stupid thing to say. I know children younger than that get killed in accidents every day.'

Yeah, Harry thought. Or, if not killed, left with life-changing injuries, even if they weren't picked up at first. His own little sister was proof of that. He pushed the thought and the guilt away. *Not now.* He needed to concentrate on his patient's bereaved mother.

'It's just…you never think it's going to happen to your own. You hope and you pray it never will.' She sighed. 'I know he was a grown man, but he'll always be my little boy.'

Harry went out to his office to call Mr Pryor to break the bad news, while Isla took over his job of holding Mrs Pryor's hand and letting her talk. On the way to his office, Harry asked one of the team to clean Jonathan's face and prepare him so his parents wouldn't have to see the full damage caused to their son by the crash. And then he went back to the relatives' room to join Isla and Mrs Pryor, staying there until Mr Pryor arrived, twenty minutes later. The Pryors clung together in their grief, clearly having trouble taking it all in. But finally, Mr Pryor asked brokenly, 'Can we see him?'

'Of course,' Harry said.

He and Isla took the Pryors through to the side room where Jonathan's body had been taken so they could see their son in private. They stayed for a few minutes in case the Pryors had any questions; then Isla caught Harry's eye and he gave the tiniest nod of agreement, knowing what she was going to say.

Then Isla said gently to the Pryors, 'We'll be just outside if you need us for anything.'

'Thank you,' Mrs Pryor said, her voice full of tears.

Outside the side room, Isla said to Harry, 'I'll finish up here—you'll be needed back in Resus.'

'Are you sure?' he asked. He was needed back in Resus; but at the same time he didn't think it was fair to leave Isla to deal with grieving parents all on her own.

She nodded. 'I'm sure.'

He reached out and squeezed her hand, trying to ignore the tingle that spread through his skin at her touch—now really wasn't an appropriate time. 'Thank you. You were brilliant. And even though I know you're more than capable of answering any questions the Pryors might have, if you need backup or want me to come and talk to them about anything, you know where to find me.'

'Yes. Those poor people,' she said softly.

'This is the bit of our job I really wish didn't exist,' Harry said.

'I know. But it does, and we have to do our best.' She squeezed his hand back, and loosened it. 'Off you go.'

He wrote up the paperwork, and headed back to Resus. To his relief, the next case was one that he could actually fix. The patient had collapsed, and all the tests showed Harry that it was a case of undiagnosed diabetes. The patient was in diabetic ketoacidosis; Harry was able to start treatment, and then explain to the patient's very relieved wife that her husband would be fine but they'd need to see a specialist about diabetes and learn how to monitor his blood sugar, plus in future they'd have to keep an eye on his diet to suit his medical condition.

Mid-afternoon, Harry actually had a chance to take his break. He hadn't seen Isla back in Resus since leaving her with the Pryors, so he went in search of her; he discovered that she was doing paperwork.

'Hey. I'm pulling rank,' he said.

She looked up. 'What?'

'Right now, I really need some cake. And I think, after the day you've had, so do you. So I prescribe the hospital canteen for both of us.'

'What about Josie?'

Harry smiled. 'She's already had her break and is in cubicles right now, but I'm going to bring her some cake back. You can help me pick what she'd like.'

For a moment, he thought Isla was going to balk at being alone with him; then she smiled. 'Thanks. I'd like that.'

'Let's go,' he said. 'We have fifteen minutes. Which is just about enough time to walk to the canteen, grab cake, and chuck back a mug of coffee.'

She rolled her eyes, but stood up to join him.

'How were the Pryors?' he asked softly when they were sitting at the table in the canteen with a massive slice of carrot cake and a mug of good, strong coffee each.

'Devastated,' she said. 'But they got to spend time with their son and I explained that he didn't suffer in Resus—that the end was quick.'

'Yeah,' he said with a sigh. 'I hate cases like that. The guy still had his whole life before him.' And something else had been bugging him. 'He was only five years younger than I am.' The exact same age as one of his siblings. And he'd had to fight the urge to text every single one of his siblings who was old enough to drive to say that they were never, ever, *ever* to ride a motorbike.

'He was three years younger than me,' Isla said.

It was first time she'd offered any personal information, and it encouraged him enough to say, 'You were brilliant with the Pryors and I really appreciate it. I assume you had a fair bit of experience with bereaved relatives when you worked in your last emergency department?'

'Actually, no.'

He blinked at her. 'How come?'

'I wasn't in an emergency department, as such—I was a nurse practitioner in a GP surgery. I retrained in Glasgow and then came here,' she said.

Something else he hadn't known about her. 'You retrained to give you better opportunities for promotion?' he asked.

'Something like that.'

She was clearly regretting sharing as much as she had, and he could tell that she was giving him back-off signals. OK. He'd take the hint. He smiled at her. 'Sorry. We're a nosey bunch at the London Victoria—and I talk way too much. Blame it on the sugar rush from the cake.'

'And on having a rough day,' she added. 'So you've always worked in the emergency department?'

'Pretty much. I trained in London; I did my foundation years here, with stints in Paediatrics and Gastroenterology.' Because of what had happened to Tasha, his first choice had been Paediatrics. He'd been so sure that it was his future. 'But, as soon as I started in the Emergency Department, I knew I'd found the right place for me. So I stayed and I worked my way up,' he said.

'Thirty-two's not that old for a special reg,' she said thoughtfully. 'Though I've already seen for myself that you're good at what you do.'

Funny how much her words warmed him. He inclined his head briefly. 'Thank you, kind madam.'

'It wasn't meant to be a compliment. It was a statement of fact,' she said crisply.

He grinned. 'I like you, Isla. You're good for my ego. Keeping it in check.'

She actually smiled back, and his heart missed a beat. When she smiled, she really was beautiful.

'I've known worse egos in my time,' she said.

'And you gave them just as short shrift?'

'Something like that.'

He looked at her. 'Can I ask you something?'

'That depends,' she said.

'Why haven't you come to any of the departmental nights out?'

'Because they're not really my thing,' she said.

'So you don't like ten-pin bowling, pub quizzes or pizza.' He paused. 'What kind of things do you like, Isla?'

'Why?'

'Because you've only been at the London Victoria for a couple of weeks, you've told me that you retrained to come here, and I'm assuming that you don't really know anyone around here. It must be a bit lonely.'

Yes, she was lonely. She still missed her family and her friends in the Western Isles hugely. And, even though she was trying to put her past behind her, part of her worried about socialising with her new colleagues. It would be too easy to let something slip. And then their reaction to her might change. Some would pity her; others would think there was no smoke without fire. And neither reaction was one she wanted to face.

She didn't think Harry was asking her out— he'd already made it clear he thought his reputation wasn't deserved—but it wouldn't hurt to make things clear. 'You're right—I don't know many people in London,' she said softly. 'And I could use a friend. *Just* a friend,' she added. 'Because I'm concentrating on my career right now.'

'That works for me,' Harry said. 'So can we be friends?'

'I'd like that,' she said. Even if his smile did make her weak at the knees. Friendship was all she was prepared to offer.

'Friends,' he said, and reached over to shake her hand.

And Isla really had to ignore the tingle that went through her at the touch of his skin. Nothing was going to happen between them. They were colleagues—about to be friends—and that was all.

CHAPTER THREE

WHEN ISLA WENT into the staffroom that morning for a mug of tea, Harry was the only one there. He was staring into his mug of coffee as if he was trying to lose himself in it. She knew that feeling well—she'd been there herself only a few months ago, when her life had turned into a living nightmare—and her heart went out to him.

'Tough shift so far?' she asked, gently placing her hand on his arm for a moment.

'No—yes,' he admitted. Then he grimaced. 'Never mind. Forget I said anything.'

It wasn't like Harry Gardiner to be brusque. The doctor she'd got to know over the last month was full of smiles, always seeing the good in the world.

He also hadn't quite lived up to his heartbreaker reputation, because since Isla had known Harry he hadn't actually dated anyone. He'd even turned down a couple of offers, which was hardly the act of the Lothario that the hospital rumour mill made him out to be. Maybe he'd told her the truth when he'd said he wasn't a heartbreaker.

Right now, something had clearly upset him. Though she understood about keeping things to yourself. Since the day that Andrew Gillespie had made that awful accusation and her fiancé had actually believed him, she'd done the same. Keeping your feelings to yourself was the safest way. 'OK,' she said. 'But if you want to talk, you know where I am.'

'Thanks.' But Harry still seemed sunk in the depths of gloom. He was still serious when he was working in minors with her, not even summoning up his store of terrible jokes to distract a little boy whose knee he had to suture after Isla had cleaned up the bad cut.

By mid-afternoon, she was really worried about him. To the point of being bossy. 'Right. I'm pulling rank,' she said. 'You need cake, so I'm dragging you off to the canteen.'

'Yes, Sister McKenna,' he said. But his eyes

were dull rather than gleaming with amusement. And that worried her even more.

Once they were sitting in the canteen—where she'd insisted on buying lemon cake for him—she asked, 'So are you going to tell me what's wrong?'

He said nothing; but she waited, knowing that if you gave someone enough space and time they'd start talking.

Except he didn't.

'Harry, either you've suddenly become a monk and taken a vow of silence as well as chastity, or something's wrong.'

He looked at her. 'How do you know I'm chaste?'

She met his gaze. 'According to the hospital rumour mill, you haven't dated in a month and everyone thinks you must be ill.'

'They ought to mind their own business.' He scowled. 'I'm not ill. I just don't want to date.'

Fair enough. She could understand that; it was how she felt, too.

'And the silence?' she asked.

He sighed. 'I don't want to talk about it here.'

So there *was* something wrong. And she liked Harry. She hated to think of him being miserable. And maybe talking to her would help him. 'After work, then? Somewhere else, somewhere that people from round here aren't likely to be hanging round to overhear what you're saying?'

There was a gleam of interest in his eyes. 'Are you asking me on a date, Sister McKenna?'

'That I'm most definitely not,' she said crisply. But then she softened. 'We're friends, Harry, and friends support each other. You look upset about something and you've been a bit serious at work lately, so something's obviously wrong. If you want to go for a drink with me after work or something and talk, then the offer's there.'

'I could use a friend,' he said. 'But you never socialise outside work, Isla. And isn't someone waiting at home for you?'

'I'm single, as well you know.'

He wrinkled his nose. 'I didn't mean that.'

'I don't follow.'

'Maybe you have a child,' he explained, 'or a relative you're caring for.'

'Is that what people are saying about me? That

because I don't go on team nights out, I must be a single parent with babysitting problems?'

He winced. 'People get curious. But I haven't been gossiping about you.'

Given what he'd said about the hospital rumour mill, she believed him. 'Just for the record, I don't have a child, and I don't look after anyone. There's just me. And that's fine.'

'Not even a goldfish or a cat?'

'No.' She would've loved a dog, but it wouldn't be fair to leave a dog alone all day. Hospital shifts and pets didn't mix that well, unless you were in a family where you could share the care. Not to mention the clause in the lease of her flat saying that she couldn't have pets. 'You know what the old song says about not being able to take a goldfish for a walk.'

'I guess.' He paused. 'Thank you, Isla. I'll think of somewhere and text you. Shall we meet there?'

She knew exactly what he wasn't saying. Because, if they travelled to the pub or café together, someone was likely to see them and start speculating about whether they were seeing each other.

Harry obviously didn't want to be the centre of gossip, and neither did she. 'Deal,' she said.

After his shift finished, Harry texted Isla the address of the wine bar and directions on how to find it.

Funny, she was the last person he'd expected to take him under her wing. She didn't date, whereas he had the not-quite-deserved reputation of dating hundreds of women and breaking their hearts. He'd been at the London Victoria for years and she'd been working there for just under a month. And yet she'd been the only one in the department who'd picked up his dark mood; and she'd been the only one who'd offered him a listening ear.

Harry didn't tend to talk about his family.

But maybe talking to someone who didn't know him that well—and most certainly didn't know any of the other people involved—might help. A fresh pair of eyes to help him see the right course of action. Because this wedding was really getting under his skin and Harry didn't have a clue why it was upsetting him so much. It wasn't as if his father hadn't got remarried before. So why, why, *why* had it got to him so much this time?

Harry was already halfway through his glass of Merlot when Isla walked into the wine bar, looked round and came over to his table. 'Hi.'

'Hi. You look lovely. I've never seen you wearing normal clothes instead of your nurse's uniform.' The words were out before he could stop them and he grimaced. 'Sorry. I wasn't hitting on you.'

Much.

Because he had to admit that he was attracted to Isla McKenna. That gorgeous creamy skin, her dark red hair, the curve of her mouth that made her look like the proverbial princess just waiting to be woken from her sleep by love's first kiss...

He shook himself mentally.

Not now.

If he told Isla what was going through his head right now, she'd walk straight out of the bar. And it would take God knew how long to get their easy working relationship back in place. He didn't want that to happen.

'You look odd without a white coat, too,' she

said, to his relief; clearly she hadn't picked up on his attraction to her and was just responding to his words at face value.

'Let me get you a drink. What would you like?' he asked.

'I'll join you in whatever you're having.' She gestured to his glass.

'Australian Merlot. OK. Back in a tick.'

Ordering a drink gave him enough time to compose himself. He bought her a glass of wine and walked back to their table, where she looked as if she was checking messages on her phone. 'Everything OK?' he asked.

'Yes.' She smiled at him. 'I'm just texting my mum, my sister and my brother to tell them I've had a good day.'

'You miss your family?' he asked.

She nodded. 'Sometimes the islands feel as far away as Australia.'

'The islands?' he asked, not sure what she meant.

'The Western Isles,' she said.

So she was from the Outer Hebrides? You couldn't get much more different from London, he thought: mountains, pretty little villages and the sea, compared to the capital's urban sprawl and the constant noise of traffic.

'It isn't that bad really,' she said. 'I can fly from here to Glasgow and then get a flight to Lewis, or get the train from Glasgow to Oban and catch the ferry home.'

But the wistfulness in her tone told him how much she missed her family. Something he couldn't quite get his head round, because he often felt so disconnected from his own. And how ironic that was, considering the size of his family. Eight siblings, with another one on the way. OK, so he didn't have much in common with his two youngest half-brothers; but he wasn't that close to the ones nearest his own age, either. And he always seemed to clash with his middle sister. Guilt made him overprotective, and she ended up rowing with him.

'But we're not talking about me,' she said before he could ask anything else. 'What's wrong?'

'You're very direct,' he said, playing for time.

'I find direct is the best way.'

He sighed. 'Considering how much you clearly

miss your family, if I tell you what's bugging me you're going to think I'm the most selfish person in the universe.'

She smiled. 'Apart from the fact that there are usually two sides to every story, I very much doubt you're the most selfish person I've ever met.'

There was a tiny flicker in her expression, as if she was remembering something truly painful. And that made Harry feel bad about bringing those memories back to her.

'I'm sorry,' he said. 'Look, never mind. Let's just have a drink and talk about—oh, I dunno, the weather.' Something very English, and very safe.

She laughed. 'Nice try. Iain—my brother— squirms just like you do if we talk about anything remotely personal.'

'I guess it's a guy thing,' he said, trying to make light of it and wishing he hadn't started this.

'But sometimes,' she said gently, 'it's better out than in. A problem shared is a problem halved. And—' she wrinkled her nose. 'No, I can't think of any more clichés right now. Over to you.'

Despite his dark mood, Harry found himself smiling. He liked this woman. Really, really liked her. Which was another reason why he had to suppress his attraction to her. He wanted to keep her in his life instead of having to put up barriers, the way he normally did. 'I can't, either.' He blew out a breath. 'I hate talking about emotional stuff. And it's easier to talk when you're stuffed with carbs. They do fantastic pies here, and the butteriest, loveliest mashed potato in the world. Can we talk over dinner?'

'Pie and mash.' She groaned. 'Don't tell me you're planning to make me eat jellied eels or mushy peas as well.'

'Traditional London fare?' He laughed. 'No. For vegetables here I'd recommend the spinach. It's gloriously garlicky.'

'Provided we go halves,' she said, 'then yes. Let's have dinner. As friends, not as a date.'

Why was she so adamant about not dating? He guessed that maybe someone had hurt her. But he also had the strongest feeling that if he tried to focus on her or asked about her past, she'd shut the conversation down. 'Deal.'

Ordering food gave him a little more wriggle room.

But, once their food had been served and she'd agreed with him that the pie was to die for, he was back on the spot.

Eventually, he gave in and told her. Because hadn't that been the point of meeting her this evening, anyway? 'My dad's getting remarried,' he said.

'Uh-huh. And it's a problem why exactly?'

'Speaking like that makes you sound like Yoda.'

She gave him a narrow-eyed look. 'Don't try to change the subject.'

'You're a bossy lot, north of the border,' he muttered.

'And you Sassenachs have no staying power,' she said with a grin. 'Seriously, Harry, what's wrong? Don't you like his new wife-to-be?'

Harry shrugged. 'I don't really know her that well.'

'So what is it?'

'This is going to stay with you?' he checked.

She rolled her eyes. 'Of course it is.'

'Sorry. I didn't mean to accuse you of being a gossip. I know you're not. I don't…' He blew out a breath. 'Well, I don't tend to talk about my personal life.'

'And I appreciate that you're talking to me about it now,' she said softly.

He sighed. 'Dad wants me to be his best man.'

'And you don't want to do it?'

'No. It'd be for the third time,' Harry said. 'And I really don't see the point of making such a big song and dance about the wedding, considering that in five years' time we'll be going through the exactly same thing all over again.'

She said nothing, just waited for him to finish.

He sighed again. 'My father—I don't know. Maybe it's a triumph of hope over experience. But this will be his seventh marriage, and this time his fiancée is younger than I am.'

His father's seventh marriage? Seeing that many relationships go wrong would make anyone wary of settling down, Isla thought. 'Maybe,' she said softly, 'your father hasn't found the right woman for him yet.'

'So this will be seventh time lucky? That'd go down really well in my best man's speech. Not.' He blew out a breath. 'Sorry. I didn't mean to be rude to you or take it out on you.' He grimaced. 'My father's charming—that is, he can be when it suits him. He can be great company. But he has a seriously low boredom threshold. And I can't understand why none of his wives has ever been able to see the pattern before she actually married him. Well, obviously not my mum, because she was the first. But every single one after that. Get married, have a baby, get bored, have an affair, move on. Nothing lasts for Dad for more than five years—well, his last one was almost seven years, but I think Julie was the one to end it instead of Dad. Or maybe he's slowing down a bit now he's in his mid-fifties.' Harry sighed. 'I really liked Fliss, his third wife. Considering she had to deal with me as a teenager...' He shrugged. 'She was really patient.'

'Did you live with your dad when you were growing up?' Isla asked.

Harry shook his head. 'I stayed with him for the occasional weekends, plus a week or so in the long school holidays. I lived with my mum and my three half-sisters. My mum also has a marriage habit, though at least she's kept husband number four.' He paused. 'Maybe that's it. Dad only has sons—six of us. Maybe he's hoping that his new wife is carrying his daughter.'

Isla added it up swiftly. Harry was one of nine children, soon about to be ten? And he'd said something about his mum being his father's first wife. 'I take it you're the oldest?'

He nodded. 'Don't get me wrong. I like my brothers and sisters well enough, but there's a whole generation between me and the littlest ones, so we have absolutely nothing in common. I feel more like an uncle than a brother.' He gave her a thin smile. 'And let's just say the best contraception ever is to get a teenager babysitting for their younger siblings. I definitely don't want kids of my own. Ever.'

'Remind me to tell my brother Iain how lucky he is that he only had me and Mags tagging around after him,' she said.

'You're the baby of the family?' he asked.

'Yes, and I'm thoroughly spoiled.'

He scoffed. 'You're far too sensible to be spoiled.'

'Thank you. I think.' She paused. 'Right. So you don't want to be the best man and you don't want to go to the wedding. I'm assuming you're trying not to hurt anyone's feelings, so you could always say you can't make the wedding due to pressure of work. That we're really short-staffed and you just can't get the time off.'

'I've already tried that one,' Harry said. 'Dad says my annual leave is part of my contract—he's a lawyer, by the way, so I can't flannel him—and he says they can always find a locum or call in an agency worker to fill in for me. Plus he gave me enough notice that I should've been able to swap off-duty with someone months ago to make sure I could be there.'

'How about a last-minute illness? Say we had norovirus on the ward and you came down with it?' she suggested.

'Norovirus in the middle of summer?' He wrinkled his nose. 'Nope. That one's not going to fly.'

'You have other medics in your family, then?' she asked.

'One of my sisters is a trainee audiologist. But everyone knows that norovirus tends to be at its worst in the winter. All the newspapers make a big song and dance about emergency departments being on black alert at the peak of the winter vomiting virus season.' He sighed. 'I've thought about practically nothing else for weeks, and there just isn't a nice way to let everyone down.'

'So the kind approach isn't going to work. Have you tried telling any of your brothers that you don't want to go?'

He nodded. 'Jack—he's the next one down from me.'

'What did he say?'

'He thinks I should be there to support the old man. So does Fin—he's the next one down from Jack.'

'And how old are they?'

'Dad's kids are all spaced five years apart. So Jack and Fin are twenty-seven and twenty-two, respectively,' he explained. 'The odd one out will be the new baby, who'll be seven years younger than Evan—he's the youngest.'

'OK. So you have to go to the wedding. But what about this best man business? Isn't there anyone else who could do it? Does your dad have a best friend, a brother—or, hey, he could always be different and have a woman as his best man if he has a sister,' she suggested.

To her relief, that actually made Harry crack a smile. 'Best woman? I can't see Auntie Val agreeing to that. She says Dad's the male equivalent of a serial Bridezilla.' He took another sip of Merlot. 'Uncle Jeff—Dad's brother—has done the duty twice, and so has Marty, his best friend.'

'So if the three of you have all done it twice, what about your next brother down? Or the youngest one? Could it be their turn?'

'I could suggest it.' He paused. 'But even if I can be just a normal wedding guest instead of the best man, it still means running the gauntlet of everyone asking me how come I'm not married yet, and saying how I ought to get a move on and settle down because I'm ten years older now than Dad was when he got married the first time, and that means I'm totally on the shelf.'

'Apart from the fact that men are never described as being on the shelf, you would still've been a student medic at twenty-two,' Isla pointed out. 'And, with the crazy hours that junior doctors work, you wouldn't have had the time to get married or even spend that much time with your new wife back then.'

'But I'm not a student or a junior doctor now. In their view, I have no excuses not to settle down.'

'Maybe you could take a date to the wedding?' she suggested.

That would be Harry's worst nightmare. Taking a date to a family wedding implied that you were serious about taking the relationship further; then, when it was clear you didn't want to do that, someone would get hurt. But Isla clearly meant well. 'I guess it would be a start—but it wouldn't stop the questions for long. They'd want to know how we met, how long we'd been dating, how serious it was, when we were planning to get engaged...' He rolled his eyes. 'They never stop.'

'So what would stop the questions?' she asked. 'What if you told them you're gay?'

'Nope. They'd still want to meet my partner. It's not the gender of my partner that's the issue—it's the non-existence.' He sighed. 'What would stop them? A hurricane, if it started raining fishes and frogs... No, that still wouldn't stop the questions for more than five minutes.' He blew out a breath. 'Or maybe I could invent a fiancée. And she isn't coming to the wedding with me because...' He wrinkled his nose. 'Why wouldn't she be with me?'

'She's working?' Isla suggested.

He shook his head. 'They'd never believe it. Same as the norovirus idea. The only way they'd believe I was engaged was if I turned up with my fiancée in tow.'

'And I'm assuming that you don't have anyone in your life who's even close to being a fiancée?'

No.

But, now he thought of it, that wasn't such a bad idea. If there was someone he could convince to go with him. Someone safe. Someone who wouldn't get the wrong idea. Someone *sensible*.

'That's a good point,' he said. 'She wouldn't have to be a real fiancée.' He smiled as he warmed to his theme. 'Just someone who'd go to the wedding with me and stop all the endless questions. Enough to keep everyone happy and nobody gets hurt.'

'Lying is never a good idea,' Isla said, grimacing.

'Hey—you suggested it.'

'Forget it. I was being flippant. It's a stupid idea.'

'Actually, I think it's a great one. And it won't be a lie. Just a teensy, tiny fib to shut everyone up. Not even a fib, really: it'd be more of an exaggeration,' Harry said. 'And if anyone asks me afterwards about setting a date, I can say that my fiancée and I realised we were making a mistake, had a long talk about it and agreed to call it all off.' He smiled. 'And my fake fiancée will know all this up front, so it'll be just fine. She won't be expecting me to marry her.'

'Do you have someone in mind?'

Someone safe. Who wouldn't get the wrong idea. Who didn't have a partner to make things complicated. And the person who ticked all those boxes just so happened to be sitting right opposite him.

Would she do it?

There was only one way to find out.

He looked straight at her. 'What are you doing, the weekend after next?'

CHAPTER FOUR

'LET ME GET this straight.' Isla's eyes were the most piercing shade of blue Harry had ever seen. 'You want me to go to this wedding with you— as your fake fiancée?'

It was the perfect solution to his problem. And she'd sort of suggested it in the first place. 'Yes.'

'No.'

'Why not? Because you're on duty and it'd be awkward to swap shifts with someone without explaining why and setting the hospital rumour mill going?'

'No, actually, I'm off duty that weekend.'

'Then what's the problem?' He frowned. 'You're exactly the right person to ask.'

'How?' she scoffed.

'Because if I ask anyone else to come to the wedding and meet my family, they'll have expec-tations,' he explained. 'They'll think that meeting my family means that I want a relationship with them. But you—you're different. You don't date. So you'll understand that I'm only asking you to come with me to the wedding to take the heat off me and stop my family nagging me to death about settling down, not because I'm secretly in love with you and want to spend the rest of my life with you.'

'That's crazy, Harry.' She shook her head. 'As I said, I was being flippant when I suggested it. You can't possibly go to a wedding and pretend you're with someone when you're not.'

'Why not?'

'Because you'll be lying to your family.'

'No, I'll just be distracting them a little,' he corrected. 'Isla, I'm asking you because I'm desperate.'

'Did you hear what you just said?' Her voice was so soft; and yet at the same time there was an edge to it.

And he could see why. He could've phrased it a lot better. He winced. 'I don't mean desperate as in…' He shook his head to clear it. 'I'm digging myself an even deeper hole, here. What I mean,

Isla, is that I need a friend to support me through a day I'm really not looking forward to. A friend I can trust not to misinterpret my intentions.'

'We barely know each other,' she pointed out. 'For all you know, I could be a psychopath.'

'Ah, now that I *am* clear about,' he said. 'I've spent a month working with you. I've seen you with patients. You're kind—you're tough when you need to be and you don't shy away from difficult situations, but overall you're kind and you're sensible and you're...' He floundered for the right word. 'Well, you're nice.'

'Nice.' She sounded as if he'd just insulted her.

'I like you. Enormously. Which is why I'm asking you—because I can trust you,' he said. 'You're safe.'

'We'd still be lying to your family.'

'A white lie. Something to keep them all happy, so their attention stays on the wedding instead of on me.'

'Nobody's ever going to believe I'm your fiancée.'

'Of course they are. If we keep the story to as near the truth as possible, it'll be convincing. We work together—and as far as they're concerned I fell in love with you as soon as I met you. You're a…what's the Scottish equivalent of an English rose?'

'I have no idea. A thistle?'

Hmm. She definitely sounded prickly right now.

'They won't buy it.' She rolled her eyes. 'I bet you normally date glamorous women. And I'm hardly the type who'd be scouted for a modelling agency.'

'You're a bit too short to be a model,' he agreed. 'But if you were six inches taller, you could be.'

She scoffed. 'It's not just my height. I'm not thin enough, either.'

'You're not fat by any stretch of the imagination. You have curves. Which isn't a bad thing.' Apart from the fact that now he was wondering what it would be like to touch said curves. How soft her skin would be under his fingertips. And she was strictly off limits, so he couldn't allow himself to think about that. 'Any of my family would take one look at you and think, yes, she's exactly the type Harry would fall for. Beautiful hair, beautiful skin, beautiful eyes, a kissable mouth.'

And now he'd said way too much. She was looking thoroughly insulted.

'It's not just about looks,' he said, guessing that was the problem—he knew his sisters hated being judged on what they looked like rather than who they were. 'As soon as they talked to you they'd think, yes, she's bright and sparky and not afraid to speak her mind, so she's perfect for Harry. He's not going to get bored with her. You've got the whole package, so it's totally believable that I'd fall for you.'

She lifted her chin. 'I'm not looking for a relationship.'

'I know, and neither am I. What I'm looking for right now is a friend who'll help me out of a hole and humour my family for a weekend.'

'So it's suddenly gone from a day to a weekend?' she asked, sounding horrified.

'It's in Cornwall, which means it's a five-hour drive from here—and that's provided we don't get any hold-ups on the motorway. The wedding's on Saturday afternoon. We can drive up first thing in the morning, stay overnight in the hotel, and then drive back on Sunday at our leisure. Which is far better than spending at least ten hours stuck in a car, as well as going to a wedding.' He blew out a breath. 'And I know it's a bit of a cheek, asking you for two days of your precious off-duty. I wouldn't ask unless I was...'

'Desperate?' Her voice was very crisp and her accent was pronounced.

'Unless I could think of any other way out of it,' he corrected. 'Or if I could think of someone else who was single but who wouldn't misunderstand my motivation for asking her to be my plus-one for the wedding.' He sighed. 'Look, forget I asked. I don't want to ruin our working relationship. I like you and respect you too much for that, and I haven't meant to insult you. This whole thing about the wedding has temporarily scrambled my brains. You're right. It's crazy. Let's pretend we never had this conversation.' He gave her a grim smile. 'I'll just man up, go to the wedding, and do what I always do about the nagging—ignore it.' He looked away. 'My next brother down is married, and the brother below him is engaged. Maybe that'll be enough to distract them all.' Though, more likely, it would give everyone more ammunition. If Jack and Fin could find someone and settle down, why couldn't he?

Though he knew the answer to that. He didn't believe in love. Not with the number of divorces he'd seen. The first one had been his parents, when he was five; then two more for his mum, and five more for his dad. That was all the proof Harry needed that marriage and settling down didn't work out for his family.

Isla looked at Harry. He'd said he didn't want to go to his father's wedding. Was it really that unreasonable of him to want someone to go with him—someone who wouldn't give him a hard time about his marital status? And to ask someone who he knew wouldn't misinterpret the request as his way of suggesting a serious relationship?

Then again, he was asking her to lie. Something she really didn't agree with. But she hadn't told Harry why she had such a thing about lying. About what had happened on the island: that her fiancé's stepfather ruined her life. He'd made a totally untrue complaint about her to her boss, which of course had been investigated. Any complaint against a member of the practice—even if it wasn't true—had to be considered seriously.

Even though she'd been completely exonerated of any wrong-doing, half the island had still believed that it must've been a cover-up. Andrew Gillespie was charming, popular, and employed a lot of people locally. What possible reason would he have had to lie?

She knew the answer to that. And if she'd told the full truth it would've blown his life apart—and there would've been collateral damage, too. People she really cared about would've been badly hurt. The gossip would have spread like wildfire, and done just as much damage.

But what had really hurt her was that Stewart had believed Andrew's lie. The one man she'd expected to be on her side… And he'd let her down. He hadn't backed her. At all.

She took a deep breath. 'Let me think about it.'

Harry's face brightened. 'You'll do it?'

'I said I'll *think* about it,' she corrected. And

maybe she could find a compromise. Something that meant Harry could have her company at the wedding but without lying about it.

'Thank you. I appreciate it. And, if you do decide to go with me, I'd be more than happy to buy you a dress or whatever.'

'That's nice of you,' she said, 'but it really won't be necessary. Apart from the fact that I can afford to buy my own clothes, thank you very much, my wardrobe consists of a wee bit more than just my uniform and jeans.'

He laughed. 'That's what I like about you. You always tell it straight.'

'There's no point in doing otherwise.'

He smiled. 'Agreed.'

'So now can we change the subject?'

Isla thought about it late into the evening when she got home to her flat. She liked Harry's company; and weddings usually meant good food, good company and dancing, all of which she enjoyed. She was seriously tempted to go with him.

And that was exactly the reason why she should say no.

It would be all too easy to get involved with Harry, and she didn't want a relationship. Neither did he. And she really felt for him. Why did his family put so much pressure on him to settle down? Why couldn't they see him for who he was—a gifted doctor who was fantastic with patients?

Her own family had always supported her and valued her. They'd stuck up for her and done their best to squash the rumours that Andrew Gillespie had started. And, when it was clear that the whispers weren't going to go away and she was going to have to leave, they'd backed her. So Isla found it hard to understand why Harry's family didn't support him.

Or was it that he didn't let them close enough to support him? Had his determination to avoid his parents' mistakes and string of broken marriages made him push them away?

She decided to sleep on it.

And she was still mulling it over on her way to work, the next morning.

Not that she had a chance to discuss it with Harry during the day. He was rostered on cubicles while she was busy in Resus, spending the morning helping to stabilise a teenage girl who'd been knocked over crossing the road while she was so busy texting her boyfriend that she didn't see the car coming. The girl had a broken pelvis, her left leg and arm were broken in several places, she had internal bleeding, and the team had to fight hard to control it before she was able to go up to the operating theatre and have the bones fixed by the orthopaedics team. The afternoon was equally busy, with two heart attacks and a suspected stroke, though Isla was really glad that in all three cases there was a positive outcome and the patients were all admitted to the wards to recover.

By the time her shift was over, Harry had already left the hospital, though he'd also left a text message on her phone asking her to call him or text him when she'd come to a decision.

If she said no, she'd feel guilty about tossing him to the wolves.

If she said yes, she'd be lying. Something she didn't want to do. Someone else's lies had wrecked her engagement, and then she'd ended up leaving the job she loved and moving hundreds of miles away to make a new start.

But Harry was trying to keep his family happy, not trying to get his own way and prove how much power he had. Which was a very different category of lying from Andrew Gillespie's. It still wasn't good, but it wasn't meant maliciously. It meant Harry could let his family down gently.

Or maybe just having someone go with him to the wedding would be enough. They didn't necessarily have to pretend to be a couple, did they?

She picked up her phone and called him.

The line rang once, twice, three times—and then the voicemail message kicked in. Not even a personalised one, she noticed: Harry had left it as the standard bland recorded message saying that his number was unavailable right now, so please leave a message or send a text.

'It's Isla,' she said. 'Call me when you're free.'

It was another hour and a half before he returned the call.

'Hi. Sorry I didn't pick up—I was playing squash,' he said. 'How was Resus today?'

She liked the fact that he'd thought enough to

ask her about her day rather than going straight in to asking whether she'd made a decision. 'Full-on,' she said, 'but all my patients survived, so it was a good day. How was cubicles?'

'Good, thanks.' He paused. 'I take it you were calling about my message?'

'Yes.' She took a deep breath. 'I've thought about it. A lot. I don't like lying, Harry. I can't go to the wedding with you as your fiancée.'

'Uh-huh.' His tone was perfectly composed and so bland that she didn't have a clue what he was thinking. 'I understand. And thank you for at least considering it. I appreciate that.'

Then she realised he thought she was turning him down. 'No, I'll go with you, Harry,' she said.

'So you've just changed your mind?' He sounded confused.

'No. I mean I'll go to the wedding with you, but as your friend—not as your fiancée.' She paused. 'That'll be enough to keep the heat off you, without us having to lie.'

'You'll actually go with me? Really?' He sounded faintly shocked, and then thrilled. 'Isla—thank you. I really appreciate it. And if there's ever a favour you want from me in return, just name it and it's yours.'

'It's fine,' she said.

'And I meant what I said about buying you an outfit for the wedding.'

'Really, there's no need. Though I could do with knowing the dress code.'

'The usual wedding stuff,' he said. 'It's a civil do. Just wear something pretty. Oh, and comfortable shoes.'

'Comfortable shoes don't normally go with pretty dresses,' she pointed out.

'They need to, in this case. The reception involves a barn dance.'

'A barn dance?'

'Don't worry if you've never done that kind of thing before—they have a guy who calls out the steps. Actually, it's a good idea because it makes everyone mix, and you get to dance with absolutely everyone in the room.'

Did he really think she'd never been to that sort of thing before? 'I'm Scottish,' she reminded him with a smile. 'In the village where I lived back on the island, we used to have a ceilidh every third Friday of the month.'

'That,' he said, 'sounds like enormous fun.'

'It was.' And she'd missed it. But the last couple she'd gone to had been miserable, with people staring at her and whispering. In the end she'd made excuses not to go. 'Is there anything else I need to know? What about a wedding present?'

'I've already got that sorted,' he said. 'So I guess it's just timing. I thought we could wear something comfortable for the journey—just in case we get stuck in traffic, with it being a summer Saturday—and get changed at the hotel.'

And that was another issue. If he'd been expecting to take her to the wedding as his fake fiancée, did that mean he expected her to share a room with him? 'Won't all the rooms already be booked? So I might have to stay at a different hotel.'

'Dad block-booked the hotel. You'll have your own room,' he said.

'Thank you.' So at least there wouldn't be any misunderstandings there. That was a relief.

She'd had enough misunderstandings to last her a lifetime.

'All I need now is your address, so I know where to pick you up,' he said.

She gave him the address to her flat.

'Excellent. And thank you for coming with me, Isla. I really appreciate it,' he said.

The next evening, just as Isla got home from work, her neighbour's door opened.

'There was a delivery for you while you were at work,' she said, handing Isla the most gorgeous bouquet. 'Is it your birthday or a special occasion?'

Isla smiled and shook her head. 'They're probably from my family in Scotland.'

'Because you've been in London for over a month now and they're missing you? I know how they feel.' The neighbour smiled ruefully. 'I really miss my daughter, now she's moved to Oxford. I send her a parcel every week so she knows I'm thinking of her. She works so hard and it's nice to be able to spoil her, even if it is at a distance.'

'And I bet she appreciates it just as much as I appreciate these,' Isla said. 'Thanks for taking them in for me.'

'Any time, love.' The neighbour smiled at her and went back to her own flat.

Once Isla had unlocked the door and put the flowers on the table, she looked at the card. The flowers weren't from her family; they were from Harry. His message was short, to the point, and written in handwriting she didn't recognise, so clearly he'd ordered them online or by phone.

I just wanted to say thank you for helping me. H x.

How lovely. She couldn't even remember the last time she'd had flowers delivered to her. And these were utterly beautiful—roses, gerberas, irises and gypsophila.

She called him. 'Thank you for the flowers, Harry. They're lovely. You didn't need to do that, but they're gorgeous.'

'My pleasure. I hope it was OK to send them to your flat? I didn't want to give them to you at work in case it started any gossip.'

Which was really thoughtful of him. 'It's fine. My neighbour took them in for me.'

'And thank you about the best man stuff, too,' he said. 'I spoke to Dad at lunchtime and he loves the idea of Evan being his best man. Julie—Evan's mum—called me to say she thinks it's a good idea, too. It makes him feel important and that his dad isn't going to forget him, even though he no longer lives with him and Julie.'

'That's good. I'm glad.' She paused. 'That sounds like personal experience.'

'I guess it is,' he said. 'I was a bit younger than Evan when my parents split up, but I can still remember worrying that Dad would forget me if he didn't live with me, because he'd have a new family to look after.' He gave a wry chuckle. 'To Dad's credit, though, he tried to keep seeing us. Even when he was going through the screaming row stage of his marriages, Saturday mornings were reserved for his boys.'

'All of you? Or did you take turns?' she asked.

'All of us, until we'd pretty much flown the nest and were off at uni somewhere.' He gave a small huff of laughter. 'Though when I look back I was always in charge of getting us all to play football at the park, because Dad would be busy flirting with someone on the sidelines. That's how he is. Be warned, he'll probably flirt with you at the wedding.'

A cold shiver ran down Isla's spine. Andrew had flirted with her, too.

Almost as if Harry was reading her thoughts—which was ridiculous, because of course he couldn't do that—he added, 'Just take it with a pinch of salt. He doesn't mean any harm by it. He just likes flirting.'

'Right.'

'Anyway. Thanks again,' Harry said. 'See you tomorrow.'

'See you tomorrow,' she said.

CHAPTER FIVE

THE NEXT WEEK and a bit flew by. At the crack of dawn on Saturday morning, Isla packed a small overnight case; she was glad she'd kept her packing to a minimum when Harry arrived, because she discovered that there wasn't much room for luggage in his bright red sports car.

'Do they know about this car on the ward?' she asked.

'Oh, yes.' He grinned. 'And they're torn between teasing me about it and pure envy because it's such a beautiful car.' He paused. 'Do you drive?'

'Yes, though I don't have a car in London because there's no point, not with the Tube being so good.'

His grin broadened. 'I'd never drive this to work because it's much more sensible to use the Tube, but on days off... Sometimes it's nice just to go wherever the mood takes you without having to worry about changing Tube lines or how far away the train station is from wherever you want to go.' He indicated the car. 'Do you want to drive?'

'Me?' She was faintly shocked. Weren't men usually possessive about their cars? And Stewart had always hated being driven by anyone else, so she'd always been the passenger when she'd been in the car with him.

'If you'd rather not drive through London, I'll do the first bit; but, if you'd like to get behind the wheel at any point, all you have to do is tell me,' Harry said. 'She's a dream to drive.'

'You're a walking cliché, Harry Gardiner,' she said, laughing. 'The hospital heartbreaker with his little red sports car.'

He just laughed back. 'Wait until you've driven her and then tell me I'm a cliché. Come on, let's go.'

The car was surprisingly comfortable. And Isla was highly amused to discover that the stereo system in the car was voice controlled. 'Boys and their toys,' she teased.

'It's so much better than faffing around trying to find what you want to listen to, or sitting through songs you're not in the mood for,' he said. 'By the way, if you'd rather connect your phone to the stereo and play something you prefer, that's fine by me.'

'Actually, I quite like this sort of stuff,' she admitted.

'Classic rock you can sing along to.' He gave her a sidelong glance. 'Now, Sister McKenna, that begs a question—can you sing?'

'You'd never get me doing karaoke,' she prevaricated.

'I won't tell anyone at work if you sing out of key,' he promised with a grin. 'Let's do it.'

'Seriously?'

'It'll take my mind off the wedding,' he said.

'So you're still dreading it?'

'A bit,' he admitted. 'Though I guess it'll be nice to see all my brothers. We don't get together that often nowadays.' He shrugged. 'Obviously the girls won't be there, because they're not Dad's, so you'll be saved from Maisie interrogating you.'

'Maisie?'

'My oldest sister,' he explained. 'Then there's Tasha and Bibi.' He gave her a wry smile. 'There are rather a lot of us, altogether.'

'It's nice that you all get on.'

'The siblings do, though the ex-wives are all a bit wary with each other,' he said. 'Obviously there have been some seriously sticky patches around all the divorces, but things settled down again after a while. The only one of his ex-wives coming to the wedding is Julie, and that's only because Evan's too little to come on his own.'

'Uh-huh,' she said. 'OK. Put on something we can sing to.'

'A girl after my own heart,' he said with a smile, and did exactly that.

Isla thoroughly enjoyed the journey; and, after they'd stopped for a rest break at a motorway service station, she actually drove his car for a while.

'Well?' he asked when they'd stopped and he'd taken the wheel again for the final bit of the journey.

'It's great,' she said. 'I can see why you love it.'

'Told you so,' he said with a grin.

Though he stopped singing along to the music as they drew nearer to the hotel where the wedding was being held. By the time he parked the car, he looked positively grim.

She reached over and squeezed his hand. 'Hey. It's going to be fine. The sun's shining and it's going to be better than you think.'

'Uh-huh.' He didn't sound convinced, but he returned the squeeze of her hand and gave her a half-smile. 'Thank you, Isla.'

'That's what friends are for. You'd do the same for me.' And she tried to ignore the fact that her skin was tingling where it touched his. It was a completely inappropriate reaction. Even if she wanted to start a relationship with someone— which she didn't—this definitely wasn't the place or the time. 'Let's do this,' she said.

He nodded, climbed out of the car, and insisted on carrying her luggage into the hotel as well as his own.

When they reached the desk to book in, the receptionist smiled at them. 'Dr Harry Gardiner? Welcome to Pentremain Hotel. Here's your key.

You're in room 217. Second floor, then turn left when you get out of the lift.'

'There should be two rooms,' Harry said. 'Harry Gardiner and Isla McKenna.'

'I'm afraid there's only one room booked,' the receptionist said. 'But it *is* a double.'

'There must be a mistake,' Harry said. 'Dad definitely said we had two rooms.'

'I'm afraid there's only one.' The receptionist bit her lip. 'I'm so sorry. We're fully booked, so I can't offer you an alternative.'

'It's fine,' Isla said, seeing how awkward the receptionist looked and not wanting to make a fuss. 'We can sort this out later. Thank you for your help.' She forced a smile she didn't feel.

Going to the wedding with Harry was one thing; sharing a room with him was quite another. And he didn't look exactly thrilled about the situation, either.

They went to the lift and found their room in silence.

'I'm so sorry about this. I did say that we were just friends and we needed two rooms. I hope my father isn't making assumptions,' Harry said.

'Look, I'll ring round and see if I can find myself a room somewhere nearby.'

'Harry, this is your family. You ought to be the one to stay here,' Isla pointed out.

'I'm really sorry about this. Dad definitely said we had two rooms. Give me a moment and I'll find an alternative,' he said, grabbing his phone to check the Internet for numbers of nearby hotels and guest houses.

Several phone calls later, he'd established that there were no rooms available anywhere near. 'Absolutely everywhere is fully booked with holidaymakers. Which I guess you'd expect on a weekend at this time of year.' He sighed. 'OK. I'll sleep in the car.'

'You can't possibly do that!' Isla frowned at him. 'Look, it's just for one night. We can share the room.'

'In that case, I'll take the couch.'

'You're too tall, your back will feel like murder tomorrow morning.' She took a deep breath. 'Look, we're adults. We can share a bed without...' She stopped before she said the words.

Even thinking them made a slow burn start at the base of her spine. *Making love. With Harry.*

Any woman with a pulse would find Harry Gardiner attractive, and of course it would cross her mind to wonder what it would be like to be in his arms. She'd just have to make sure she didn't act on that impulse. 'Well,' she finished lamely.

'You're right. It's not as if we're teenagers,' he said. And at least he hadn't seemed to pick up on what was going through her head.

'Exactly. Now, we need to get changed,' she said briskly. 'Do you want to change in here or in the bathroom?'

'You pick,' he said.

'Bathroom,' she said, and escaped there with her dress and make-up bag.

Sharing a room with Isla McKenna.

It was the sensible solution, Harry knew.

The problem was, he didn't feel sensible. He was already on edge about the wedding, and if they shared a bed it would be all too easy to seek comfort in her.

She's your colleague, he reminded himself. Off

limits. She wants a relationship just as little as you do. Keep your distance.

He'd just about got himself under control by the time he'd changed into the tailcoat, wing-collared shirt and cravat his father had asked him to wear. He left the top hat on the bed for the time being, took a deep breath and knocked on the bathroom door. 'Isla, I'm ready whenever you are,' he said, 'but don't take that as me rushing you. There's plenty of time. I just didn't want you to feel that you had to be stuck in there while I was faffing about in the other room.'

She opened the door. 'I'm ready,' she said softly.

Harry had never seen Isla dressed up before. He'd seen her wearing jeans and a T-shirt, and he'd seen her in her uniform at the hospital. On every occasion she'd worn her hair pinned back and no make-up, not even a touch of lipstick.

Today, she was wearing a simple blue dress that emphasised the colour of her eyes, a touch of mascara, the lightest shimmer of lipstick—and she looked stunning. Desire rushed through him, taking his breath away. How had he ever thought that Isla would be *safe*? He needed to get himself under control. Now.

'You look lovely,' he said, hearing the slight croak in his voice and feeling cross with himself for letting his emotions show.

'Thank you. You don't scrub up so badly yourself, Dr Gardiner,' she said.

Exactly the right words to help him keep his burgeoning feelings under control, and he was grateful for them. 'Shall we?' he asked and gestured to the door.

'Sure.' She gave him a cheeky grin. 'Don't forget your hat.'

'No.' He glanced at her high-heeled shoes and did a double-take. 'Isla, are you going to be able to dance in those?'

'I'm Scottish. Of course I can.' She grinned. 'And if I can't I'll just take them off.'

He really, really wished she hadn't said those words. Because now there was a picture on his head that he couldn't shift. Isla, all barefoot and beguiling, standing before him and looking up with her eyes full of laughter. And himself taking off every piece of her clothing, one by one...

Get a grip, Harry Gardiner, and keep your hands and your eyes to yourself, he warned himself. He pinned his best smile to his face, and opened the door.

'Isla, this is my father, Robert Gardiner,' Harry said formally when they joined the wedding party in the hotel gardens. 'Dad, this is my friend Isla McKenna.'

Isla could see the family resemblance. Although Bertie's hair was liberally streaked with grey, clearly once it had been as dark as Harry's, and if it hadn't been cut so short it would've been as curly as Harry's, too. Bertie had the same dark eyes and same sweet smile as his son, though Harry hadn't inherited his dimples.

'It's lovely to meet you, Mr Gardiner,' she said.

'Everyone calls me Bertie,' he corrected with a smile. 'It's lovely to meet you, too, Isla—I can call you Isla?'

'Yes, of course.'

'Good.' His eyes twinkled at her. 'I believe I have you to thank for persuading Harry to be here at all, and I hear it was your idea for Evan to be my best man.'

She winced. 'Sorry, that sounds horribly like interference on my part.'

He smiled and clapped her shoulder. 'Sweetheart, it was an inspired suggestion, and you talked Harry into coming so I most definitely owe you champagne.'

For a moment, she froze. Andrew Gillespie had been just as charming and flirtatious, but he'd hidden a serpent under the smile. Then she remembered Harry's warning that his father would flirt with her but meant nothing by it. And he was right. There was nothing remotely assessing in the way Bertie looked at her. No hidden agendas. He wasn't a carbon copy of Andrew.

'Now, has my boy here introduced you to everyone?' Bertie asked.

'We've hardly had time, Dad—remember, we drove up this morning from London and we had to get changed.'

'You could've come last night and had dinner with us,' Bertie pointed out. 'But you said you were on a late shift and couldn't get anyone to swap with you.'

'Exactly.' Harry gave him a tight smile. 'I happen to work in the busiest department at the hospital, you know.'

'Hmm.' Bertie rolled his eyes. 'Come with me, sweetheart, and I'll introduce you.'

'Where's Trixie?' Harry asked.

Bertie smiled. 'Now, son, you've been to enough of my weddings to know that it's bad luck for the groom to see the bride before the ceremony.'

And then Isla finally relaxed, liking the way Harry's father was able to poke fun at himself.

The next thing she knew, she'd been introduced to a dozen or more of Harry's family, including most of his brothers. The twelve-year-old looked as if he'd rather not be there and she made a mental note to go and chat to him later; the seventeen-year-old looked a little awkward. The two oldest, Jack and Fin, seemed to be assessing her suitability for Harry.

'Sorry about that,' Harry said softly as soon as they were alone again. 'Clearly they were under instructions from Maisie. Jack's only a year and a bit older than her, and they see things pretty much the same way.'

'It's fine,' Isla said with a smile.

The wedding ceremony was held under a canopy on the clifftop, and the views were breathtaking. And seeing the sea made Isla feel suddenly homesick.

'Are you OK?' Harry asked.

'Sure. It's just been a while since I've seen the sea properly.'

'Before we go back to London,' he promised, 'we'll go for a walk on the beach.'

'I'll hold you to that. It's the one thing I regret about London—there's no sea. And I miss walking by the waves.'

'There's a beach of sorts on the Thames. I'll show you some time, if you like.'

'Thank you.'

The wedding itself was lovely. Harry's youngest brother was indeed the best man, and he handed the rings to Bertie at the altar.

Trixie and Bertie's vows were very simple and

heartfelt. Isla guessed that Harry was going to find this bit the hardest, so she slipped her hand into his and squeezed his fingers. He squeezed back and then didn't let her hand go.

After the wedding, the photographer had everyone clustering together in groups. Isla particularly liked the one of Bertie with his six sons, all of them wearing top hats and then a second shot with them all throwing their hats into the air. She took a couple of snaps on her phone for posterity.

And then the photographer called her and Harry over. 'Now, you two. Stand together here.' He posed them, then shook his head. 'I want you closer than that,' he said.

Oh, help. He was clearly under the misapprehension that she and Harry were a proper couple. Just as she had a nasty feeling that Harry's family thought that, too—even though Harry had made it clear they were just friends.

'That's it. Arms round each other,' the photographer said.

They'd have to go along with it. Making a fuss

now would make everything awkward and embarrassing.

'Look into each other's eyes,' the photographer said. 'That's it. I want to see the love. As if you're just about to kiss each other.'

Isla's mouth went dry.

Kissing Harry.

The worst thing was, she could just imagine it. Putting her hand up to stroke his cheek, then sliding her hand round his neck and drawing his head down to hers. Parting her lips. Seeing his pupils widen with desire. Feeling his lips brush against hers, all light and teasing and promising; and then he'd pull her closer, jam his mouth properly against hers and deepen the kiss...

'That's *exactly* what I'm talking about!' the photographer crowed.

Isla focussed again and saw the shock in Harry's eyes.

Had she given herself away? Or was he shocked because the same feelings had been coursing through him?

She didn't dare ask, but she made some excuse to dive back into the crowd. And please, please, let her libido be back under control before Harry could guess what she'd been thinking.

Trixie—who turned out to be a primary school teacher—clearly understood how bored the younger members of the family would find things, so she'd arranged a duck race on the stream running through the hotel grounds for them. Evan insisted on making a team with Harry, and made their duck into a pirate.

Harry was such a sweetheart, Isla thought; he was as patient with all the children here as he was in the emergency department. And yet he'd been so adamant about not wanting children of his own. She couldn't quite work it out.

'He's very good with children,' Bertie said, joining her.

'They love him at work—he has this stock of terrible jokes to distract them,' Isla said with a smile.

'I can imagine. Half of them come from his brothers.' Bertie paused. 'So you met when you started working together?'

Isla had half expected an inquisition. And the

best way to stop the misconception being uncovered and making things really awkward would be to stick as closely to the truth as possible. 'Yes—a couple of months ago.'

'And you're a doctor, too?'

'No, I'm a nurse,' Isla said.

'Senior nurse, actually.' Harry came up and slung one arm casually around Isla's shoulders, clearly having worked out what was going on. 'Let's have the inquisition over now, please, Dad.'

'If you actually told me things, Harry,' Bertie grumbled good-naturedly, 'then I wouldn't have to pump other people for information, would I?'

'I'm a doctor. I'm used to keeping things confidential,' Harry said with a grin.

'You're impossible,' Bertie said with a sigh.

'Like father, like son,' Harry said with a broad wink. 'Isla's my friend. End of story. Come on, Isla—it's time for food and I'm starving,' he added, and shepherded her into the large marquee on the lawn.

The food was wonderful: Cornish crab terrine followed by roast beef and all the trimmings, then a rich pavlova with clotted cream and raspberries, and finally a selection of traditional Cornish cheeses and crackers.

The waiters topped up everyone's glasses with champagne, ready for the speeches.

The father of the bride gave the first speech. Sticking with tradition, he welcomed the guests, thanked everyone for coming, spoke a little bit about Bertie and Trixie, and then toasted the bride and groom.

Harry murmured in her ear, 'Excuse me—I'm going to have to leave you for a minute or two.'

She realised why when little Evan stood up on his chair, with Harry crouched beside him.

'I'm Evan and I'm my daddy's best man,' Evan said proudly. 'My big brother Harry says my speech has to be funny, so I'm going to tell you my favourite joke. What did the banana say to the monkey?' He waited for a moment before delivering the punchline. 'Nothing—bananas can't talk!'

Everyone laughed.

'Harry says the speech has got to be short as well as funny, so I'll stop now. Happy wedding day, Daddy and Trixie.'

Everyone echoed, 'Bertie and Trixie.'

Harry whispered something in Evan's ear and the little boy's eyes went wide. 'Harry, I forgot!'

Harry smiled at him and patted his shoulder, and mouthed, 'Go on.'

'Um, I'm sorry, everyone, I forgot the other bit. The bridesmaids look really pretty and they did a good job. You have to drink to the bridesmaids now.'

There were amused and indulgent laughs, and everyone chorused, 'The bridesmaids.'

Bertie stood up last. 'And I must say thank you to my best man, who did a fabulous job.'

'And Harry,' Evan chipped in.

Bertie grinned. 'I gather it was a bit of a team effort between my youngest and my oldest sons. But that's what family's all about. Pitching in together.' He raised his glass. 'I'd like to make a toast to my beautiful bride, Trixie, and to my wonderful family—thank you all for coming here to celebrate with us.'

Harry quietly came back to join their table at that point. Isla reached for his hand under the table and squeezed it.

After the speeches, it was time to cut the cake. 'The middle layer is chocolate,' Trixie said, 'so that should make all the men in my new family happy.'

'As sweet as you are,' Bertie said, and kissed her. 'And I believe the band is ready for us. Perhaps we could all move in to the other marquee?'

The band was set up at one end, and there were chairs lining the edges of the floor. For the first dance, the band played a slow dance; Bertie and Trixie started things off, followed by the bride and groom's parents, and then the bridesmaids and best man.

Isla wondered if Harry was going to suggest dancing with her, but at the end of the song the singer announced, 'And now it's time for you all you to dance off that cake—I want everybody up on the floor, and there's no excuse for not dancing because we're going to call the steps for you.'

There were protests from the younger members of the wedding party, but they were roundly ignored—and, by the middle of the first dance, everyone was laughing and thoroughly enjoying themselves. Isla knew most of the steps from the ceilidhs she'd been to back on the island. Her own wedding reception would've been just like this. But she pushed away the sadness; now wasn't the time or place, and she wasn't going to let the shadow of Andrew Gillespie spoil this weekend.

Harry watched Isla dancing while he was on the other side of the room. Her glorious hair flew out behind her, and she'd been telling the truth about being able to dance in high heels. Before today, he hadn't had a clue how well his colleague could dance. If the rest of the staff could see their quiet, capable, almost shy senior nurse right now...

She was sparkling, and she fitted in well with everyone. And he noticed that Isla had even managed to get his two middle brothers to join in the dancing, rather than sitting on the edge of the room, mired in teenage awkwardness. She'd actually got them laughing as they danced together. Harry already knew from working with her that she had great people skills, but this was something else. She wasn't just coping with his extended family, she was actually joining in with them.

He had a nasty feeling that Isla McKenna was the one woman who could tempt him to break his 'no serious relationships' rule. So much for asking her to come here with him because she was safe: she was nothing of the kind. And he would need to be careful, especially as they were sharing a room tonight.

And almost everyone in his family had something to say about her to him. Fin said it was about time he found someone like her; Jack pointed out how well she was getting on with everyone and how nice she was with the teenagers; Julie came over to say how much little Evan liked her and so did she.

If his family had their way, they'd be getting married next week, Harry thought moodily. And he hoped Isla wouldn't take any of it to heart. He'd told them the truth. They just didn't want to believe it, and wanted him to have the happy-ever-after.

Marriage wasn't an option he would ever seriously consider. In his world, the happiness from marriage was brief and the heartache lasted an awful lot longer.

The band had a break when the canapés and sandwiches appeared, and he managed to snatch some time with Isla.

'Oh, look at this—miniature Cornish pasties, and miniature scones with clotted cream and strawberry jam!' she exclaimed in delight. She tried a scone. 'Oh, you really have to try this, Harry,' she said, and popped a bite of scone into his mouth.

His lips tingled where her fingers had touched them.

Oh, help. He was going to have to keep himself under strict control. It would be all too easy to do something stupid—like catch her hand and kiss the back of her fingers, and then turn her hand over so his mouth could linger over the pulse at her wrist.

'This is one of the nicest weddings I've been to,' she said.

Harry pulled himself together with an effort. 'I guess it's better than I thought it would be.' The real reason that it was better for him was because she was there, but he was wary of telling her that because he didn't want her to take it the wrong way. Especially as he had a nasty feeling that it meant more to him than just the support of a friend—and, despite the fact they'd just celebrated a wedding, he knew this wouldn't last. It never did.

But he pushed the thoughts away and forced himself to smile and be sociable.

After the break, the band switched from the barn dance to more traditional wedding music. Isla danced with his two oldest brothers and Bertie, and then Harry reclaimed her.

Just as the band segued into a slow dance.

It was too late to back out now, because she was already in his arms.

Now he knew what it was like to hold her close. She was warm and soft and sweet. And it scared him, how right this felt—like the perfect fit.

He could see his father smiling approval at him. His brothers did likewise.

Oh, help. They all thought that he and Isla had been fibbing about their relationship and were a real couple—and, even though he'd originally intended that they believe that, he realised now that Isla had been right and it made things way too complicated.

They really ought to sit out the next dance. Go and talk to other people. Distract his family.

But he couldn't let her go. The next song was another slow dance, and he ended up drawing her closer and dancing cheek to cheek with her instead. He could smell her perfume, all soft and beguiling—much like Isla herself. He closed his eyes. All he had to do was turn his head towards her, just the tiniest fraction, and he'd be able to kiss the corner of her mouth. And then he'd find out if her lips were as sweet as the rest of her.

He felt almost giddy with need. It had been a long time since he'd wanted to kiss someone as much as he wanted to kiss Isla McKenna.

Giddy was about right. The mood of the wedding had clearly got to him and he needed to start being sensible, and that meant right now, before he did something they'd both regret.

He pulled away from her slightly.

'Are you OK?' she asked, her blue eyes dark with concern.

He nodded. 'I just need some fresh air.'

'I'll come with you if you like.'

He ought to say no. He really, really ought to make an excuse to put some distance between them. Not walk outside with her in the gardens under the light of a full moon.

But, despite his best intentions, he found himself saying yes, holding her hand and walking out of the marquee with her.

CHAPTER SIX

THE SKY WAS darkening and the first stars were appearing; they were so much brighter out here in the countryside than they were in London. Harry could hear the gentle, regular swish of the waves against the sand at the bottom of the cliffs and it was hypnotic, soothing his soul. He sat down on the grass next to Isla, looking out at the sea, and slid his arm round her shoulders. For a moment he felt the tiniest bit of resistance from her; then she leaned into him and slid her arm round his waist.

Funny how right it felt. Not that he was going to let himself think about that. Because he didn't do serious relationships and he valued Isla too much to mess things up between them.

They sat in companionable silence together for a while. Eventually, she was the one to break it. 'So are you really OK, Harry?' she asked softly.

'Yeah. I'm OK.' He blew out a breath. 'It's just… This whole wedding thing. It's good to see my brothers, but when I look at them I can't help remembering the times they've cried on my shoulder, convinced it was the end of the world because their mum and dad were fighting all the time, or had just split up and they had to move house and start at a new school. Every divorce caused so much damage. It uprooted the kids and made them so miserable.'

'They all seem pretty well adjusted now.'

Except him, perhaps. Not that he intended to discuss that. 'But they've still been hurt.' He sighed. 'Ten marriages between my parents. It's a bit excessive.'

'Your dad seems happy.'

'For the moment—but you can see the pattern, Isla. It's meant to be a seven-year itch, but Dad only seems to make it to four or five years before he's had enough and misses the thrill of the chase.' He shook his head. 'And I don't want to be like that, Isla. If I'm like my parents and I can't settle down… I don't want to hurt anyone.'

'And that's why you isolate yourself?' she asked.

He'd never thought about it in that way. He'd always thought about it as saving others from him repeating his parents' mistakes. 'I guess.'

She rubbed her thumb in a comforting movement against his back. 'You're pretty hard on yourself, Harry. From what I've seen today, your family loves you. Your brothers all look up to you.'

He gave her a wry smile. 'Maybe.'

She twisted her head to kiss his cheek, and heat zinged through him at the touch of her mouth against his skin. Just as much as it had when the photographer had suggested they should look in love with each other, as if they were just about to kiss.

Right at that moment he'd really wanted to kiss Isla, to see if her mouth was as soft and as sweet as it looked. Her eyes had been wide and dark, and it would've been oh, so easy to lean forward and do it. Just as he wanted to kiss her, right now.

This was a bad idea.

He knew he ought to take his arm from her shoulders, move away from her, and suggest that they go back to the marquee and join the dancing.

But he couldn't move. It felt as if they were held together by some magnetic force. Something he couldn't break—and, if he was honest with himself, something he didn't want to break.

'You're a good man, Harry Gardiner,' Isla said. 'I can understand why you avoid connecting with anyone—but you're really not being fair to yourself. You're loyal and you're kind, and I think you more than have the capacity within you to make a relationship work. To really love someone.'

He groaned. 'You sound like my mother. And my sisters.'

'If that's what they say, then I agree with them,' she said.

'Can we change the subject?' he asked plaintively.

'Because you're too chicken?'

Yes. 'No, because the sky's beautiful and I don't want to talk about something that makes me antsy.'

'Fair enough,' she said.

'You looked as if you were enjoying the dancing earlier.'

'The barn dance? Yes—it's very similar to the

ceilidhs we had on the island. That's what we were going to have for our wedding.'

Wedding?

Isla had been going to get married?

The fact that she was single—and had made it clear she intended to stay that way—meant that something must have gone badly wrong. Was that the reason that had made her leave the island? And why she'd reacted so badly to the idea of being a fake fiancée—because she'd once been a real one?

'Were?' he asked softly.

She shook her head. 'Don't worry about it. It's a long story.'

'Right now I have all the time in the world.' His arm tightened round her shoulders. 'It's not going any further than me—you've kept my confidence and I'll keep yours. Plus someone very wise once told me it's good to talk because it's better out than in. A problem shared is a problem halved, and all that.'

'Before I ran out of clichés, you mean?' she asked wryly, clearly remembering that conversation.

'What happened? Your fiancé died?' he asked quietly. It was the only reason he could think of why Isla hadn't got married.

'Stewart? No. He's still alive and perfectly healthy, as far as I know.' She blew out a breath. 'We'd known each other since we were children. I guess it all goes with the territory of living in a small community. You end up settling down with someone you've known for ever.'

He waited, giving her the space to talk.

'We started dating a couple of years ago. He asked me to marry him and I said yes. My family liked him and I thought his liked me.'

So that had been the problem? Her ex's family hadn't liked her? And yet she'd still been prepared to meet his own family today. His respect for her went up another notch.

'But then Stewart's mum asked me for a favour,' she said softly. 'According to Bridie, Andrew—Stewart's stepfather—had bit of a drink problem. She wanted me to talk to him and see if I could persuade him to get some help to stop drinking, before he ended up with cirrhosis of the liver.' She looked away. 'I was trying to help.'

'And he didn't like you interfering?'

'Partly, but Andrew got the wrong end of the stick when I asked to talk to him privately. He assumed I was interested in him and he made a pass at me.' She sighed. 'I should've handled it better. I just hadn't expected him to react in that way. I always thought his marriage to Bridie was rock-solid and he would never even think about looking at another woman.'

'It wasn't your fault, Isla. Besides, any decent man understands that if a woman says no, it means no.' Harry had a nasty feeling where this might be going. 'So he wouldn't take no for an answer?'

'Oh, he did,' she said grimly. 'But Andrew Gillespie was used to getting his own way. He really didn't like the fact that I'd said no to him. So he called the head of the practice and said that I'd behaved unprofessionally. He claimed that I'd asked to see him privately under the guise of talking about his health, and then made a pass at him.'

'What? That's appalling. I hope your boss sent him away with a flea in his ear.'

'My boss,' she said, 'had to investigate. Exactly as he was bound to do if any patient made a complaint about any of the staff at the practice.'

'But it obviously wasn't true.'

'And I was exonerated.' She blew out a breath. 'But you know all the clichés. There's no smoke without fire. Mud sticks.'

He blinked. 'Other people believed him?'

She nodded. 'I lived in a village. Everyone knew me; but everyone also knew Andrew. He was popular with the locals—partly because he employed a lot of them, and partly because he could be very charming indeed.'

'But surely your fiancé and his mum knew the truth?'

'Andrew could be persuasive as well as charming.'

Harry really didn't get this. 'But his wife asked you to have a quiet word with him and help him with his drinking problem. She knew there was more to him than met the eye. Surely she must've known that he wasn't telling the truth?'

'And there's another cliché for you: stand by your man. Even if it means upholding a lie.'

'That's…that's…' He didn't have the words. 'I don't know what to say.' But there was one thing he could do. He shifted her on to his lap and held her close. 'Best I can do right now is give you a hug.'

'Gratefully accepted.'

And, oh, he wanted to kiss her. Except that would be totally inappropriate. He couldn't suggest that they lose their worries in each other. Much as he felt that it might help them both tonight, tomorrow they'd have to face up to their actions and it would all get way too messy. So he just held her. 'I'm really sorry that you had to go through something so horrible. And I don't see how anyone who'd known you for more than ten minutes could believe that you'd ever be unprofessional, much less try it on with your fiancé's stepfather.'

'Thank you for the vote of confidence,' she said.

'I still can't get over the fact that people you'd lived with and worked with and treated thought that you were capable of that kind of behaviour. Much less your ex. And right now I don't know what to say,' he said. 'Other than wanting to punch this Andrew Gillespie guy very hard— and I know exactly where to hit him to do the most damage—and wanting to shake your ex until his teeth rattle for being such an idiot and not seeing straight away that you weren't the one telling lies.'

'Violence doesn't solve anything,' she pointed out. 'Look at all the drunks we have to patch up on a Friday and Saturday night.'

'I know, but it would make me feel better,' he said.

She smiled. 'You're not a caveman, Harry.'

'Right now I'd quite like to be. Being civilised can be overrated.'

She stroked his cheek. 'Thank you for taking my part.'

'Isla, anybody who knows you would realise the truth without having to be told. You're honest, dependable and sincere.'

'Thank you. Though I wasn't fishing for compliments.'

'I know. I'm just telling you, that's all. And I'm sorry that you had to go through such a horrible situation. Though I'm glad you chose to work at the London Victoria. And I'm also very glad you're here with me right now.' And he really understood now why she wasn't in the market for a relationship—why she'd been wary even of joining in with the team outside work. She'd been let down so badly. It would be hard to take the risk of trusting someone again.

If anyone had told Isla a month ago that she'd be sitting on Harry's lap with their arms wrapped round each other, she would've scoffed.

And yet here they were. Doing exactly that.

And she'd just spilled her heart out to him.

Odd that Stewart had known her for years and years, and yet he'd got her totally wrong; whereas Harry had known her only a few weeks and he knew her for exactly who she was. *Honest, dependable and sincere.* It warmed her heart to know that was what he thought of her.

'I'm glad I'm here, too,' she said. And, even though she knew she was skating on very thin ice indeed, she gave in to the impulse to lean forward and kiss his cheek. 'Thank you for believing in me.'

His eyes went even darker. 'Isla.' He was looking at her mouth.

Just as she was looking at his.

Was he wondering the same as she was, right now? What it would be like if their lips actually touched? Did his mouth tingle with longing, the same way that hers did—the same way she'd felt when the photographer had posed them, except this time it was just the two of them in the starlight, and it felt so much more intense?

Clearly yes, because he leaned forward and touched his mouth to hers. And it felt as if the sky had lit up with a meteor shower. His mouth was warm and soft and sweet, promising and enticing rather than demanding, and she wanted more.

She slid her hands into his hair; his curls were silky under her fingertips. And he drew her closer so he could deepen the kiss.

'We wondered if you two lovebirds would be out here,' a voice said, and they broke apart.

She felt colour flare through her cheeks as she

looked up at Harry's father and new stepmother. What on earth did she think she was doing, kissing Harry like that in the middle of the garden where anyone could see them?

'Don't say a single word,' Harry said, dragging a hand through his hair and looking as guilty as Isla felt.

'It's my wedding day and it's Cornwall, so it's meant to be romantic,' Bertie said. 'Though you weren't quite telling the truth about being just friends, were you?'

Harry groaned. 'Dad. Not now.'

'We came out to find you because Evan is supposed to be going to bed and he refuses to go without saying goodnight to you—and that's both of you, actually,' Trixie said, including Isla. She grinned. 'He likes you. We all do, Isla.'

'OK, OK, we're coming,' Harry said, and exchanged a glance with Isla. She climbed off his lap and they headed in to the marquee to say goodnight to Evan. The little boy did his best to persuade them to read him a couple of stories each, but Julie whisked him away with a promise of 'later'.

'You're a natural with kids, Isla,' Harry remarked when Evan had gone.

'Because of my job,' she said. 'And so are you.'

He laughed. 'It's my job—and probably because I have so many siblings.'

'And yet you say you don't want kids of your own, even though you're so good with them. I don't get it.'

'I just don't,' Harry said. 'And I'd rather not talk about it.'

'Fair enough.' And she hadn't told him everything about Stewart, so she was hardly in a position to nag about keeping secrets.

'Come on—they're playing your song,' Harry said as the band started playing Abba's 'Dancing Queen'.

It was a deliberate distraction, and Isla knew it, but at the same time she didn't want to push him. He'd looked as if he'd had enough soul-baring for today.

'I'm a little bit older than seventeen, you know.'

'You can still dance,' he said, and led her onto the floor.

What else could she do but join in? Especially

as this part of the band's set was cover versions of all the kind of songs that got everyone on the floor at weddings, from the youngest to the oldest.

Though Harry avoided the slow dances that were played every so often to change the mood and the tempo, she noticed. Which was probably just as well, given what had happened outside in the garden. If they'd been in each other's arms again, holding each other close, the temptation to repeat that kiss might've been too much for both of them.

At the end of the evening, they headed for their room.

'I really ought to take the couch,' Harry said.

'Because we kissed in the garden?' She took a deep breath. 'Let's blame it on the moonlight and Cornwall being romantic.'

'I guess.'

'Harry, we're adults. We've got a long drive back to London tomorrow. We both need sleep. It's not as if I'm planning to pounce on you.' Even though part of her really wanted to.

'Of course. And you're right.' He gave her a

smile, but she could see that he had to make the effort. 'Do you want to use the bathroom first?'

'Thank you.'

She lingered as long as she dared, hoping to give herself a little time to calm down. Once she'd cleaned her teeth and changed into her pyjamas, she went back into the bedroom. Harry was still dressed. 'Do you have a preferred side of the bed?' she asked.

'Whichever you don't want,' he said.

'Thanks. I like to sleep by the window,' she said. 'See you in a bit.'

When Harry came out of the bathroom, he was wearing pyjamas and Isla was in bed. It was all very civilised and proper, but underneath everything there was an undercurrent. Her mouth was still tingling in memory of that kiss. Plus this was the first time she'd shared a bed with anyone since she'd broken up with Stewart. Even though they'd both made it clear that this was going to be completely chaste, it still felt unnerving.

Particularly as part of her didn't want this to be chaste at all. And, from the way Harry had kissed her under the stars, she had a feeling that it was the same for him. Wanting the ultimate closeness—but scared it would all go wrong, and not wanting to have to deal with the resultant carnage.

'Goodnight,' he said, climbed in beside her and turned his back.

Which was the most sensible way of dealing with it, she thought. Keeping temptation well at bay. 'Goodnight,' she echoed, and turned her own back.

Isla was very aware of his closeness and it took her a while before she could relax enough to sleep. She woke briefly in the night to discover that Harry was spooned against her, one arm wrapped round her waist and holding her close. She'd really missed this kind of closeness. It would be oh, so easy to turn round and kiss him awake; but that would change everything and it wouldn't be fair to either of them. She knew he didn't want a relationship; she didn't want one either.

Even if Harry Gardiner did kiss like an angel.

She'd just have to put it out of her mind. They were colleagues and friends, and that was that.

* * *

The next morning, Harry woke to find himself spooned against Isla, with his arm wrapped round her. Her hand was resting lightly over his, as if she welcomed the closeness.

He could tell from her slow, even breathing that she was still asleep.

Oh, help.

She was all warm and soft and sweet. It would be so easy to brush that glorious hair away from her shoulder and kiss the nape of her neck, his mouth brushing against her bare skin until she woke.

And he knew she'd respond to him, the way she'd responded to his kiss in the garden last night. If his father hadn't interrupted them, he had a nasty feeling that he might've carried Isla to the bed they shared right now and taken things a whole lot further.

As in all the way further.

He took a deep breath. She'd told him about what had happened to her in Scotland, though he had a feeling that she'd left a fair bit out. Why on earth hadn't her fiancé believed in her? Surely

he'd realised that his stepfather hadn't been telling the truth? Although Isla hadn't said which
of them had broken off the engagement, Harry
knew it had shattered her faith in relationships.

So he needed to ignore his body's urging. He
had to do the right thing.

Carefully, he disentangled himself from her
without waking her, took a shower and dressed.
It was still relatively early for a Sunday morning
after a wedding reception, but they had a long
way to drive and it would be sensible to leave earlier rather than later. He made them both a cup
of tea from the hospitality tray on the dresser, set
hers on the table next to her side of the bed, and
touched her shoulder. 'Isla.'

Her eyes fluttered open. For a moment, she
looked confused, as if she wasn't sure where she
was or why someone was sharing her bedroom.
Then her eyes widened. 'Oh. Harry.'

'Good morning. I made you a cup of tea.'

'Thank you,' she said, sounding almost shy.
'What time is it?'

'Eight. I know it's a bit early.'

'But we have a long drive.'

He was relieved that she understood. 'I thought I might go for a walk before breakfast. It'll give you a chance to shower and get changed.'

She looked grateful. 'I appreciate that.'

'See you in half an hour?'

'I'll be ready and packed,' she promised.

'Yeah.' He smiled at her. So there wasn't any collateral damage from last night, then—either from the kiss or from her telling him about her past. She still looked a little shy with him, but he knew she'd won her trust. Just as she'd won his.

And, back in London, everything would be just fine.

CHAPTER SEVEN

AT BREAKFAST, LITTLE Evan was there and insisted that they join him and his mother. Isla was
amused to note that he copied Harry exactly in
everything he ate; clearly the little boy had a serious case of hero-worship where his big brother
was concerned.

When they'd finished, they said goodbye to
Harry's family, then drove back to London. It was
much quieter on the way back; there wasn't quite
an awkward silence between them, but this time
Harry was playing classical music rather than
something they could both sing along to, and Isla
didn't really know what to say. They probably
ought to discuss what had happened yesterday
and reset the ground rules, but she had the dis-
tinct impression that Harry didn't want to discuss
it and would change the subject if she raised it.

Although they stopped for lunch, Harry sug-

gested that they grabbed a burger at the motorway service station—and she noticed that this
time he didn't offer to let her drive.

She'd always been good with people, but the
way Harry was stonewalling her was unlike anything she'd ever known.

'Are you OK?' she asked.

'Sure. Just thinking about work.'

And there wasn't really an answer to that.

'Do you want to come in for coffee?' she asked
when he parked outside her flat, even though she
was pretty sure he'd say no.

'Thanks, but I've already taken up enough of
your time this weekend,' he said, equally politely.

Isla felt as if somehow she'd done something
wrong; but, if she tried to clear the air, would it
make things even worse between them?

She was beginning to see what the hospital
grapevine meant about Harry the Heartbreaker.
He was already withdrawing from her and they'd
gone to the wedding just as friends, not as part
of a date. Was he really that wary of emotional
involvement?

'Thank you for coming with me this weekend,' he said.

'Hey, that's what friends are for,' she said lightly. Though she had a nasty feeling that their burgeoning friendship had just hit an iceberg, one that could totally sink it.

Harry was still in scrupulously polite mode as he took her bag from the car and saw her to her door. 'See you at work tomorrow, then,' he said.

'Yes, see you tomorrow.'

And he really couldn't escape fast enough, she noticed. Back inside her flat, she kept herself busy by catching up with her chores, but it wasn't quite enough to occupy her full attention. She couldn't help wondering if what had almost happened between them in the moonlit garden would affect their relationship at work. Tomorrow, would Harry be his usual self with her, or would he have withdrawn even further?

She had no answer the next morning, because they weren't rostered on together; he was in Resus and she was on triage duty.

But, in the middle of the morning, a woman came in carrying a toddler who rested limply against her. She sounded utterly distraught as she begged, 'Please help me—it's my grandson. I think he's dying!'

Isla signalled to the receptionist that she'd take the case.

She swiftly introduced herself. 'I can see that you're worried, but I need you to take a deep breath and answer some questions for me so I can help your grandson,' she said gently. 'What's his name and how old is he?'

The woman's voice was quavery but her answers were clear. 'Peter Jacobs, and he's two.'

'Can you tell me what's happened, Mrs Jacobs?'

'He started being sick and his vomit was a weird colour, a kind of greyish-black. And he's drowsy—at this time of the morning he's usually really lively. I called the ambulance, but they said they'd be a while before they could get to us, so I asked my neighbour to drive us in.'

Greyish-black vomit. It flagged up alarm signals in Isla's brain. 'Do you know if he's eaten anything he shouldn't have?' she asked.

'He said something about sweeties and tasting

nasty. I couldn't think what he might have eaten, at first—I always keep any tablets in the medicine cabinet on the wall in the bathroom, and it has a child lock on it even though he can't reach it yet—but my husband's been taking iron tablets. He has arthritis in his hands so he can't use a childproof cap on his tablets. I didn't realise he'd left them in our bedroom instead of putting them back in the medicine cabinet. It has to be those—Peter hasn't been in the garden, so I can't think of anything else.'

'Do you have any idea how many tablets he might have eaten?'

Mrs Jacobs shook her head, and rummaged in her bag to produce a packet of iron supplement tablets. 'I brought these in case they'd help you. My husband can't remember how many he's taken, but it wasn't completely full. Please help us.' Her face was anguished. 'My son's never going to forgive me if anything happens to Peter.' She swallowed hard. 'If he—if he dies. I can't…'

'He's not going to die,' Isla soothed, though she knew that iron poisoning could be fatal in children. 'You did the right thing by bringing him straight here. Do you have any idea how long ago he might have taken the tablets?'

'It must have been in the last hour or two.' She bit her lip. 'Lee dropped him off just before he went to work. My daughter-in-law's away on business and Lee had to go in. I was only supposed to be minding Peter for the morning. And now…' She broke off, shuddering.

Isla squeezed her hand. 'Try not to worry. Let's go in to the department now because I need to discuss something very quickly with the doctor and then we'll treat your grandson.' She took Mrs Jacobs into Resus and beckoned Harry over.

'This is Mrs Jacobs and her grandson Peter, who's two and we think he might have accidentally eaten some iron tablets,' she said. 'Mrs Jacobs, would you like to sit here and give Peter a cuddle while I fill Dr Gardiner in on all the details?'

Mrs Jacobs looked grey with anxiety, but she did as Isla directed and sat on the bed with Peter on her lap.

'Mrs Jacobs doesn't know how many tablets he took, but she thinks it happened in the last couple of hours. The symptoms sound like iron poisoning.' She gave him a rundown of what Mrs Jacobs had told her.

'I agree—it sounds like iron poisoning.' Harry said. 'OK, we need serum iron, full blood count and glucose. Iron tablets are radio-opaque, so let's do an X-ray to find out how many tablets he took, and then we'll do gastric lavage or even whole bowel irrigation.'

Isla knew that activated charcoal couldn't absorb iron, so bowel irrigation was the most effective treatment, but it was going to be an unpleasant experience for the little boy and even worse for his grandmother. 'I know she's going to be worried about her grandson, but I think we should advise her to stay in the relatives' room while we treat him.'

'Agreed. Let her go with you to the X-ray,' Harry said, 'but then it's hot sweet tea and wait for us to finish.'

They went over to the bed where Mrs Jacobs was sitting with her grandson. 'Peter, I'm Dr Harry and I'm going to try and make you better,' Harry said.

The little boy clearly felt too ill to smile, let alone respond verbally.

Harry turned to the boy's grandmother. 'Mrs Jacobs, we're going to run some blood tests and give him an X-ray to see if we can get a better idea of how many iron tablets he's taken; then we'll be able to treat him. I know this is going to be hard for you, but while we're treating him I'd like you to wait in the relatives' room.'

'Why can't I stay with him? He doesn't know anyone here and he'll be frightened,' Mrs Jacobs said.

'It'll upset you more to see the treatment than it'll upset Peter to be with us, especially as he's quite groggy,' Harry explained. 'I promise we'll do our best for him, and we'll come and get you so you can be with him again as soon as he's stable.'

She looked distraught. 'My son's never going to forgive me.'

Forgiveness. Yeah. Harry knew all about that. His mother and Tasha had forgiven him for that awful afternoon, but he'd never been able to forgive himself. Even now he still woke up in a cold sweat, having relived the whole thing in his dreams. Seeing his little sister tumble all the way down the stairs, and everything felt as if it was in super-slow motion—and, whatever he did, he just couldn't stop it happening. And then she lay there on the floor, not moving…

Except his dream was always that bit worse than real life. The worst and ultimate might-have-been. In his dream, Tasha never woke up. In real life, thank God, she had.

Mrs Jacobs bit her lip. 'I thought I'd been so careful. I've got cupboard locks and those things you put on the door to stop it slamming on their little fingers. I never thought he'd go into our bedroom and take those tablets.'

Just as Harry had never thought that Tasha would follow him up the stairs. He gave her a rueful smile. 'You can never predict anything with toddlers—and I'm sure your son will forgive you. You'd be surprised what children will forgive their parents.' *And their brothers.*

Mrs Jacobs didn't look convinced.

'You made a mistake, and you'll know in future to keep everything locked away,' Isla said.

'We'll do our best to make sure he's going to be absolutely fine. Do you want someone in the department to call your son for you?'

Mrs Jacobs shook her head. 'No, that wouldn't be fair on him. I'll do it.'

'OK,' Harry said, and squeezed her hand. 'Try not to worry too much, and this will take a while.'

'You can come with me to the X-ray department, so he won't be scared,' Isla said, 'and then I'll show you to the waiting room. Peter, sweetheart, I'm Nurse Isla, and I'm going to help Dr Harry look after you and make you better.'

She took Peter and Mrs Jacobs to the X-ray department, then showed the older woman where to wait. By the time Isla came back to Resus, Harry already had the X-ray up on his screen.

'There seem to be a dozen tablets,' he said. 'So we'll need to do a whole bowel irrigation.'

It was an unpleasant and lengthy procedure, but between them they managed to get rid of the iron tablets and stabilise Peter's condition.

'Shall I go and fetch his grandmother now?' Isla asked as they transferred the little boy to the recovery room.

'Good idea,' Harry said. 'The poor woman must be worried sick.'

Isla went into the relatives' room to see Mrs Jacobs. There was a man with her who bore enough family resemblance for Isla to guess that he was Peter's father.

They both looked up as she walked in. 'Is he all right?' they asked in unison.

'He's going to be absolutely fine,' Isla said, 'and you can come in to the recovery room to see him and have a word with Dr Gardiner.' She looked at the man. 'I assume you're Peter's father?'

'Yes. I couldn't believe it when Mum called me.'

'I'm sorry,' Mrs Jacobs said. 'And I promise you nothing like this will ever happen again while I'm looking after him.'

'He could've *died*,' Mr Jacobs said, his voice cracking.

'But he didn't,' Isla said gently, resting her hand on his arm for a moment in sympathy, 'and accidents happen. The most important thing is that Peter's all right—and the scariest part is over now.'

She took them through to the recovery room,

where Mr Jacobs put his arms round his son and held him tightly. The little boy was still groggy, but mumbled, 'Daddy, Peter got poorly tummy.'

'I know, baby. I love you,' Mr Jacobs said, 'and you're going to be all right.'

'Want Mummy,' Peter said tearfully.

'Mummy will be home soon,' Mr Jacobs said, 'and I'm not going to leave you until she's back. You're safe.'

The little boy snuggled against his father. And oh, how Harry never wanted to be in that position again. Worried sick about a small child whose injuries could've been fatal.

'Mr Jacobs, this is Dr Gardiner,' Isla said.

'Peter's going to be fine,' Harry said. 'I assume your mum already told you that he accidentally ate some iron tablets.'

'Dad should never have left his tablets where Peter could see them,' Mr Jacobs said, his voice tight. 'I can't believe he was so stupid.'

'Peter isn't the first toddler who's eaten tablets thinking that they were sweets and he won't be the last,' Harry said calmly. 'No matter how careful you are, accidents happen, and your mother did exactly the right thing in getting Peter straight here.'

What a hypocrite he was, telling this man that accidents happened and to forgive his mother. Because Harry had never been able to forgive himself for Tash's accident. Not after they discovered that the damage was more permanent than concussion and a broken arm. 'We irrigated his bowel to get rid of the tablets.'

'Oh, my God—that sounds horrific!' Mr Jacobs said, looking shocked.

'It's more effective at getting rid of the tablets than giving him an emetic, and it's also less risky,' Isla said.

'But he'll have nightmares about it.' Mr Jacobs bit his lip. 'My poor boy, having to go through all that.'

'He probably won't remember any of it. He's very young and was quite groggy when he came in,' Harry reassured him.

'So can I take him home now?' Mr Jacobs asked.

'No—because he's so young we want to admit him to the children's ward for the next twenty-four hours, so we can keep an eye on him,' Isla explained.

'So he could get worse?' Mrs Jacobs asked, her face full of fear.

'The early symptoms have settled now, but they sometimes come back the day after, so we always play it safe with young children and keep an eye on them,' Harry said. 'We can take you up to the children's ward and introduce you to the team, and they have facilities for parents or grandparents to stay overnight.'

'I can't believe...' Mr Jacobs shook his head as if to clear it. 'Oh, my God. If I'd lost him...'

'He's going to be fine,' Isla reassured him. 'I know it's easy for me to say, but try not to worry.'

Harry was glad she'd been the one to say it. Those particular words always felt like ashes in his mouth when the patient was a child.

She took the Jacobs family up to the children's ward and helped them settle in, then headed back down to the Emergency Department. She'd missed her lunch break, so she grabbed a coffee in the staff kitchen and topped it up with cold water so she could drink it more quickly. She knew she could grab a chocolate bar from the vending machine on the way back to the triage team, and that would keep her going to the end of her shift.

Isla was halfway through her coffee when Harry walked in, holding two packets of sandwiches and two cans of fizzy drink. 'I guessed you wouldn't have time for lunch, either, so I nipped out to the sandwich stall by the hospital shop and grabbed these for us. They didn't have a huge choice but there's tuna mayo or chicken salad. You get first pick.'

'Thank you,' she said, feeling a huge surge of relief. Harry was behaving just as he had before they'd gone to Cornwall—which meant that the weekend hadn't damaged their working relationship after all. She hadn't realised quite how worried she'd been about it until she felt the weight leaving her shoulders. 'Why don't we split them and have one of each?'

'Sounds good to me,' he said.

'The kettle's hot. Do you want a coffee?'

He indicated the drinks. 'I'll get a quicker caffeine hit from this. I bet you put cold water in that coffee, didn't you?'

'Yes,' she admitted.

He grimaced. 'I prefer my coffee hot, thanks all the same. Do you want one of these cold drinks?'

'I'll stick with my half-cold coffee, but thanks for thinking of me,' she said. 'How much do I owe you for the sandwich?'

He flapped a dismissive hand. 'It's your shout, next time. That was a good call with young Peter.'

'I feel for his grandmother,' Isla said. 'She was trying her best, and accidents happen. Her son was so angry with her.'

'His dad probably feels guilty because he wasn't there to stop it happening, and that's why he was so angry,' Harry said. He blew out a breath. 'And that's another reason why I don't ever want to settle down and have children. You can't do a job like this and give enough attention to your kids.'

Plenty of other hospital staff managed it, Isla thought. Harry was letting his family background colour his judgement. But it wasn't her place to argue with him. 'Mmm,' she said noncommittally, and ate her sandwich. 'I'd better get back to the triage team.'

'And me to Resus. See you later.'

'Yeah.' She smiled at him. 'Thanks again for the sandwich.'

It was a busy week in the department. Isla wasn't looking forward to being rostered on cubicles on Saturday night; she hated having to pacify the more aggressive drunks, who seemed to take the hospital's zero tolerance policy personally and it made them even more aggressive with the staff.

She knew that having to deal with aggressive patients was par for the course for the shift, but her heart sank when she saw her patient at one o'clock in the morning; the guy had clearly been in a fight. As well as the black eye and lacerations to his face, there was what looked like a bite on his hand; either he'd hit the other man very hard on the mouth, in which case there might well be a tooth embedded within the bite, or the other guy had just bitten him anyway.

Damping down her dismay, she reminded herself that she was a professional.

'How long ago did this happen, Mr Bourne?' she asked.

'I've been waiting here for hours, so you tell me,' he asked, curling his lip.

Great. Drunk and aggressive, and not in the mood for giving information. She suppressed a sigh.

'I thought you lot had to see us within a certain time?'

'We have targets,' she said, 'but we have to treat the more urgent cases first. That's why we explain to patients that they might have to wait, and someone who came in after them might be seen first because their condition is more urgent.'

'Huh.' He swore enough to make his opinions about that very clear.

'I need to examine your hand, Mr Bourne. May I?'

He held his hand out for her to take a look. Thankfully, she couldn't see any foreign bodies in the wound. 'The good news is your hand isn't broken,' she said when she'd finished examining his hand, 'and there doesn't seem to be any joint involvement. As it's a puncture wound, there's more risk of it developing a bacterial infection, so I need to clean it thoroughly before you go. But it won't hurt because I'll do it under local anaesthetic. Can you remember the last time you had a tetanus injection?'

He shrugged and pulled a face. 'Dunno. Maybe when I was at school.'

'OK. I'll play it safe and give you a tetanus shot as well.'

He took one look at the needle before she anaesthetised his hand and was promptly sick.

''S not the drink. 'M not good with needles,' he slurred.

'It's OK,' she said. 'I'll clean it up when I've finished treating you.' She numbed the skin around the bite, irrigated it thoroughly, and had just turned away to get scalpel from the trolley to debride the ragged edges of the wound when she felt her bottom being roughly squeezed.

Unbelievable.

She turned round and glared at him. 'That's not appropriate behaviour, Mr Bourne. Don't do it again. And may I remind you that we have a zero tolerance policy here?'

'Oh, come on, love.' He leered at her. 'Everyone knows what you naughty nurses are like beneath that starched uniform.'

'You're here as my patient,' she said firmly, 'and nothing else. Just to make it very clear, Mr Bourne, I'm not interested, and I don't want you to touch me like that again. Got it?'

'You don't mean that. You know you want—'

But the man broke off his blustering when the curtain suddenly swished open.

Harry stood there, his arms folded and his face grim. 'Problem, Sister McKenna?'

She just nodded towards the patient.

'There's no problem, Doc,' Mr Bourne slurred. 'She's just being a tease, that's all. Playing hard to get.'

Isla had been here before, thanks to Andrew Gillespie. Another drunk, though he'd had more of a civilised veneer. Anger flashed through her; she was half tempted to be totally unprofessional and smack the guy over the head with one of the stainless steel bowls on the trolley.

But then she went ice cold. She'd told Harry some of what had happened with Andrew back on the island. And this case was oh, so similar. Would he think that Isla had been lying to him, and her two accusers were telling the truth after all? That she was a tease and she'd asked for it? Would he, like Stewart, refuse to back her?

'Playing hard to get? Absolutely not,' Harry said, his voice filled with contempt. 'That's complete and utter rubbish.'

Relief flooded through her. It wasn't going to be like before, then. Harry was going to back her. And she was shocked by how much she'd wanted him to believe her.

'We have a zero tolerance policy in this department,' Harry said, 'and that includes both verbal and physical abuse of the staff. Sister McKenna is here to treat you—and if you continue abusing her and touching her without her consent, then you'll leave the hospital without any treatment.'

Mr Bourne clenched his fists. 'And you'll make me, will you?'

'You're drunk,' Harry said. 'You've thrown up everywhere and you're barely capable of standing, so it wouldn't be hard for security to escort you out.'

'Too scared to do it yourself?' Mr Bourne taunted.

'No, too busy tending to people who need help,' Harry said. 'Don't try and play the tough nut, because I'm not interested. I'm here to do a job, not to bolster your ego. By the look of your hand, if we don't treat you, it'll be infected by the morning and it's going to hurt like hell—so it's your choice. You can apologise and let us do our job, or you can leave now and risk a serious infection. Your call.'

'I could sue you.'

'You could try,' Harry said, 'but who is a judge going to believe? Two professional medics, or someone who's too drunk to use his judgement?'

This could escalate very quickly, Isla thought. And if that comment about needles had been the truth rather than bravado, maybe there was a quick way of stopping Mr Bourne in his tracks. 'You'll need antibiotics,' she said, and took the largest syringe from the trolley.

The drunk went white when he saw it.

She quickly put a bowl into his hands. 'If you're going to throw up again, please try and aim for this. If you're sick over your hand, I'll have to clean it out again.'

He retched, but thankfully the bowl remained empty.

'Is there something you'd like to say to Sister McKenna?' Harry asked coolly.

'Sorry,' Mr Bourne mumbled.

'Good. And I don't want another word out of you unless it's to answer a question.' Harry turned to Isla. 'Sister McKenna, I'll stay with you to make sure this man doesn't make a nuisance of himself.'

'Thank you,' she said. 'And now I can get on with my job.' She finished debriding the wound. 'Because this is a bite wound, Mr Bourne,' she said, 'I can't put stitches in it straight away as there's a greater risk of infection. You'll need to go and see your family doctor or come back here in three or four days and we'll stitch it —then.' She put a sterile non-sticky dressing over it and looked at Harry. 'Given that it's a hand wound involving a human bite, should we use prophylactic antibiotics?'

'Good idea,' he said. 'I'll prepare the syringe for you.'

'And a tetanus shot, please,' she said.

'But you're the doctor,' the drunk man mumbled, staring at Harry as he drew up the medication. 'Not supposed to take orders from a nurse.'

'I told you I didn't want another word out of you,' Harry reminded him, 'and for your information Sister McKenna is a senior nurse and is more than qualified to do all of this. I'm only here as a chaperone because you were behaving like an idiot. I suggest you treat the staff here with the respect they deserve.'

'Sharp scratch,' Isla said cheerfully, and administered the tetanus shot.

Mr Bourne whimpered.

'And another,' she said, and gave him the antibiotics. 'I don't expect you'll remember what I say to you right now,' she said, 'so I'll give you a leaflet to back it up. Go to your family doctor or come back here in three or four days to have that wound stitched. If the skin around the wound goes red, swollen and tender, or you get a temperature, then you need to see someone straight away as it means you have an infection. But hopefully the antibiotics should prevent that happening in the first place.' She handed him the leaflet. 'Is anyone waiting for you outside?'

'Nah. The mate who brought me here will've gone home by now or his missis'll be in a snit with him, snotty cow that she is.'

'Then I'll leave you to make your own way out of the department,' she said.

He grimaced, got to his feet and lumbered off.

'I'm pulling rank,' Harry said. 'Staff kitchen, right now.'

Isla shook her head. 'I need to clean this place up first.'

'Then I'll help you,' he said, and did exactly as he promised.

When all the vomit had been cleaned up and the cubicle was fit for use again, he said softly, 'No more arguments. Staff kitchen.'

She nodded and went with him in silence.

He put the kettle on. 'I'm making you some hot, sweet tea. Are you all right?' he asked.

'Thanks, but I really don't need tea. I'm fine.'

'Sure? Apart from the fact that his behaviour

was totally unacceptable, that must've brought back—'

'I'm fine,' she cut in, not wanting to hear the rest of it. Memories. Yeah. It had brought them back. But she wasn't going to let it throw her. 'And thank you for coming to the rescue.'

'Which any of us would do if any colleague was dealing with a difficult patient. You don't have to put up with behaviour like that.'

'Not just that,' she said softly, 'you believed me. You backed me.'

He smiled. 'Isla, apart from the fact that I know you well enough to be absolutely sure you'd never do anything unprofessional or encourage patients to grope you, the guy stank of stale booze and vomit—not exactly female fantasy material, was he?'

'I guess.'

Harry grimaced. 'And his attitude to women stank even more.'

She nodded. 'Just a bit.'

'Are you really sure you're OK?' he asked.

'Yes. But thank you for asking.'

He patted her shoulder. 'Any time.'

Heat zinged through her at his touch; and how inappropriate was that? Especially given that he'd just had to rescue her, and he'd said that she would never do anything unprofessional.

She could do with a cold shower.

Or an injection of common sense.

'I really don't need any tea, and it's heaving out there. We'd better get back to work. See you later,' she said. And she walked away before she said something needy or stupid. Harry Gardiner had made it very clear that he was off limits, and she'd promised herself she wouldn't get involved with anyone again.

And that was non-negotiable.

CHAPTER EIGHT

HARRY WAS WAITING for Isla when she came off duty after the handover.

'I'm seeing you home,' he said.

'Thank you, but there's no need,' she said.

'Actually, there is. You had a rotten shift.' He paused. 'And I'd just feel a bit happier if I saw you home and made you a bacon sandwich.'

'Tough. I don't have any bacon.'

'Then we'll do plan B,' he said. 'I know a very nice café not far from here where they do the best bacon sandwiches ever. And a bacon sandwich with a mug of tea is the best answer to a rubbish shift.'

'You're not going to give up, are you?' she asked.

He smiled. 'Nope.'

'A bacon sandwich would be nice,' she admitted, 'but I'm buying. To say thanks for rescuing me earlier.'

'Am I allowed to buy us a mug of tea, then?'

'I guess so.' She smiled at him.

They walked to the café together, where they ordered bacon sandwiches and a large pot of tea with two mugs.

'Thanks again for rescuing me,' she said.

'I'd do the same for any colleague who was being hassled by a patient,' he said.

'I don't mean just that—we'd all step in—but the fact that you believed me.'

'Of course I did,' he said softly. 'But that's why I wanted to have breakfast with you this morning. Because I don't want the behaviour of a stupid, thoughtless patient ripping open some fairly recent scars.'

'It did, a bit,' she admitted. 'It made me remember the look on Andrew's face when I turned him down, and then how my life suddenly went into quicksand mode.' And it was still her biggest fear: that someone would make another false accusation against her, that even though she was exonerated people would still think she'd done something wrong, and she'd have to pick up the wreckage of her life all over again.

Harry reached across the table and squeezed her hand. 'I know you had a tough time on the island, but that's not going to be repeated here,' he reassured her. 'Apart from the fact that every single person in our department knows you're totally professional, the guy was drunk and obnoxious.' He paused. 'There's more to it than that, isn't there?'

She sighed, suddenly too tired to hold it in any more. 'I was so scared you wouldn't back me.'

'Of course I'd back you! You're my colleague and my friend.' He frowned, as if remembering something. 'But you said your ex didn't back you when his stepfather lied about you. Why not?'

She sighed. 'I guess for him there were only two possibilities. One was that I was a faithless liar who was trying to cheat on him with his stepfather and was lying even more about it to save my own skin when I'd been found out. The other was that I was telling the truth, and the man who'd brought him up since he was two and treated him as if Stewart was his biological son rather than his adopted son was capable of cheating on Stewart's mother.'

'But surely he knew you well enough to know that you'd never cheat on him—that you weren't the liar?'

'That's what I'd hoped, but I was wrong,' she said sadly. 'I suppose he went for the lesser of two evils. For him, it was better to think that he'd made a mistake and picked the wrong person than to think that his mother had made a bad choice and could end up being hurt. Bridie had already had enough unhappiness in her life, with Stewart's dad being killed at sea when Stewart was only six months old. Andrew had made everything all right again. Stewart needed to believe that it was still going to be all right.'

'Even though that meant not believing you?'

'As I said, it was the lesser of two evils.' She bit her lip. 'I had hoped that, once he'd got over the shock, he'd see I was telling the truth and we'd work it out. But it was obvious he didn't want to see it. Then again, even if he had seen it, I'm not sure I would ever have managed to get past the feelings of being betrayed. How could I spend the rest of my life with someone who didn't be-lieve me? What would happen the next time we had a difference of opinion—would he take my part, or would he assume that I was lying?' She looked away. 'So I broke it off.'

'Did Stewart know that Andrew had a drink problem?'

'I don't know. I guess Andrew could be very plausible and, if Bridie was colluding with him to keep the situation from everyone...' She sighed. 'Probably not.

'And you didn't tell Stewart the truth?'

'How could I? Breaching patient confidenti-ality is totally unprofessional—and doing that would've meant that Andrew's accusations were true, at least in part. Plus Bridie and Andrew could've denied that he had a drink problem. And that in turn would make Stewart and everyone else think that either I was lying to save my-self, or that I was perfectly happy to gossip about something that a patient had told me in strictest confidence.'

'So whatever you did, you couldn't fix the situation—someone would end up being hurt. That's a horrible situation to be in.'

'It wasn't much fun at the time,' she said wryly. 'At least my family and close friends believed me.'

'But the gossip still drove you away from the island?'

'I was going to tough it out. But every day I had to face the same kind of speculation. Every day I had patients who didn't want to see me because they'd lost their trust in me. Every day I found I couldn't do my job properly because all the lies and the gossip were getting in the way. After three months of it, I wasn't sleeping or eating properly because I was so miserable. Which is when my parents, my brother and my sister sat me down, told me they loved me and they believed in me. They said basically I could stay on the island and let my soul wither away a little more every day, or I could leave and retrain and recapture the joy in what I did for a living.'

'And that's why you chose to work in the emergency department? Because you'd still be helping people, but they wouldn't know you and you wouldn't know them, and there wouldn't be any cradle-to-the-grave stuff?'

'Which is ironically why I became a nurse practitioner in the first place,' she said. 'But yes. And I like my job in the emergency department. I do.'

'But you miss your family.'

'I'm a big girl. I'll cope. And,' she added sadly, 'you might want to have it all, but in the end I guess you have to make some sacrifices and learn to compromise. That's life.'

'I guess,' he said. 'But in your shoes I'd be really angry about it.'

'I was,' she said, 'but I'm pretty much over the anger now. I'm just sad it worked out that way.'

'And then some idiot who's drunk out of their mind starts behaving in the same way towards you.'

'There is that,' she admitted.

'And because the guy had beer goggles on, he clearly assumed everyone else did, too.'

'Beer goggles?' She wasn't with him.

'When you've drunk enough beer to think that whoever you see is more attractive than they are.

Except in this case he was right about you and wrong about himself,' Harry explained.

'Even sober and not covered in his own vomit, he wouldn't have been my type,' Isla said with a grimace.

'That's a cue to ask what your type is,' Harry said, 'except I wouldn't quite dare.'

'And I wouldn't answer,' Isla said crisply. Because she wouldn't dare tell Harry Gardiner that he was exactly her type. Not just because he was easy on the eyes, but because he was a genuinely nice guy and she liked the way he treated other people. She just wished he'd be a bit kinder to himself.

He laughed. 'And that's my cue to top up our mugs of tea.' He released her hand. 'Seriously, though, I was worried about you. We all have things in our career that make us flinch when we come across a similar case later on.' He always hated dealing with toddler falls. Especially serious ones. Not that he planned to tell Isla about that. Instead, he said, 'For me, it's a ruptured abdominal aortic aneurysm.'

'You lost the patient?' she asked.

'Yup. On my very first day in the emergency department. It was very nearly my last,' Harry said. 'I mean, I know statistically we lose more patients in our department than any other, simply because of the nature of the job. But I wasn't prepared to lose someone on my first day. She was the same age as my grandmother—in fact, she even looked like my grandmother. Masses of fluffy grey curls, carrying a little bit too much weight. She came in with back pain.' He blew out a breath. 'She was sweating, tachycardic and hypotensive. I thought it might be a ruptured abdominal aortic aneurysm, but she didn't have any mottled skin on her lower body and, because she was overweight, when I examined her I couldn't be sure that there was a pulsatile abdominal mass. I went to see my special reg to ask for a second opinion and some advice on what I should do next, but by the time we got back to my patient she'd collapsed and the nurse was calling for the crash team. And then we lost her. I went home after my shift and cried my eyes out, then I rang my grandmother and begged her to get herself checked out properly and go on a diet.'

'Oh, Harry.' Her sympathy showed in her expression, too.

'Going in to work the next day was awful. How did I know I wouldn't kill off any more patients?' He shrugged. 'I seriously thought about giving up medicine.'

'Harry, you didn't kill your patient. You were young and inexperienced, and you did the right thing—you knew you were in over your head and you went to get help rather than blundering on.'

'I still should've thought harder about what I was doing. I should've had a much lower threshold of suspicion and got the portable ultrasound.'

'Even then, you probably couldn't have saved her,' Isla pointed out. 'You know as well as I do that a ruptured aortic aneurysm has a really high mortality rate and a lot of patients don't even make it to hospital.'

'I knew that with my head,' Harry said, 'but my heart told me otherwise.'

'But you got through your next shift?'

'Yes. Actually, the senior sister on the ward was a real sweetheart. She gave me a hug when I came in, told me that I'd been unlucky to have such a bad first day in the department, and that I was to put it out of my head. And then she said I was rostered in Resus.' He blew out a breath. 'I was terrified that I'd kill another patient. But I saved someone. A toddler who'd had a severe allergic reaction to eggs. The paramedics had already given her adrenaline, but she got worse on the way to the emergency department and I had to intubate her and stabilise her. And that's when I realised what our job was all about. You do your very best to save someone. Sometimes you can't, and some patients are very difficult to help—but as long as you know you've done your very best then that's enough.'

That was true. But he hadn't done his best with Tasha, had he? He'd left the stair gate open and assumed she wouldn't follow him. And he wasn't going to put himself back in a situation where so much would be at risk—not ever, ever again.

When they'd finished their breakfast, Harry insisted on walking Isla home.

She paused at her front door. 'I guess that bacon

sandwich revived me a bit. Would you like to come in for a coffee?'

Part of Harry wanted to back away. After all, he'd told Isla some pretty personal stuff in the café. Plus he had a nasty feeling that this thing between them was drawing nearer and nearer towards a proper relationship, the one thing he'd always sworn to avoid—and actually going in to her flat was another step towards that.

But his mouth clearly wasn't working in sync with his brain, because he found himself saying, 'Thanks, I'd like that.'

'Come and sit down and I'll put the kettle on. Decaf?'

'If I'm to get any sleep this morning, then yes please,' he said with a smile.

She ushered him into her living room and bustled off to the kitchen. Her flat was neat and tidy, just as he'd expected.

The mantelpiece in her living room was full of framed photographs. There was one of Isla on her graduation day with two people who were obviously her parents, as he could see the resemblance to both of them; a couple of weddings that he guessed were her older sister and her brother, given that Isla was the bridesmaid and again he could see a resemblance; and others which were obviously christening photographs.

And the look of sheer love on her face as she was holding the babies told him everything: Isla was the sort who wanted to settle down and have a family. Right now she was still getting over the way her ex had let her down, but Harry thought that these photos were a warning sign that he really shouldn't start anything with her because they wanted completely different things out of life. Things that weren't compatible.

They'd talked about compromising, but this was one area where he just couldn't compromise. He didn't want to be responsible for a child. Given his genes, if he tried to make a go of it with Isla and actually got married, there was a fair chance they'd end up divorced—and if they'd had a child, that would mean shattering another life. He didn't want to put a child through the kind of hurt he'd been through when he was smaller. And he didn't want to hurt Isla, either.

So he needed to back off.

Right now.

Which was exactly what he'd been doing since the wedding…until that drunk had groped Isla and claimed that she'd started it. Harry really couldn't have left her to deal with that on her own, especially because he knew it had happened to her before. And he'd been thinking with his heart rather than his head when he'd taken her for breakfast and seen her safely back here.

He was just about to stand up, go to the kitchen and make some excuse to leave when Isla came through with two mugs of coffee and a tin of biscuits, which she put down on the small coffee table in the centre of the room.

Too late.

He'd have to stay long enough to drink his coffee, or it'd be rude and he'd upset her. And he wanted to let her down *gently*.

Small talk. That was what would save the situation. 'Nice flat,' he said.

'I like it,' she said. 'It's light and airy, and although it's a bit on the small side it's convenient for work.'

He managed to keep the small talk going for

just long enough to let him gulp down his coffee. Then he yawned and said, 'I really ought to leave and let you get some sleep. I need some myself or I'll be nodding off all through my shift tonight.'

'I know what you mean,' she said with a smile. 'See you later. And thanks again.'

'No problem,' he said.

And when he left her flat, he gave himself a pep talk all the way home. Back off. Keep your distance. And stop wanting something you definitely can't have.

CHAPTER NINE

HARRY WAS DISTANT with Isla that night at work; she would've put it down to them both being busy, but he didn't ask her to eat with him or have coffee together at their break.

They didn't see each other while they were off duty on Monday and Tuesday, but he was distant with her for the next couple shifts they worked together.

Something had obviously happened, but Isla couldn't work out what she'd said or done to upset him. He'd been so lovely with her when the drunk had upset her; he'd backed her on the ward, and then he'd made her feel safe and secure by having breakfast with her and walking her home. But, now she thought about it, he'd started going distant on her when she'd made him a mug of coffee, back at her flat.

She really needed to clear the air and find out

what she'd done so she didn't repeat it. She valued him as a friend and a colleague and she didn't want anything spoiling that.

Was it the shadow of Andrew Gillespie? Harry had said he believed her, but was he having second thoughts now, the way so many people on the island had back then?

At the end of their shift on Friday, Isla waited to catch Harry. 'Hey. I was thinking, maybe we could go for a drink somewhere.'

'Sorry, I can't.' He gave her an apologetic smile. 'I'm supposed to be playing squash. League match.'

Why did that feel like a made-up excuse? she wondered. 'Harry, I think we need to talk,' she said quietly. 'I've obviously done something to upset you and I'd like to clear the air. Can we meet after your squash game, maybe?'

He didn't look her in the eye and his tone was a little too breezy for her liking when he said, 'You haven't upset me at all.'

'So why have you been keeping as much distance as you can between us, this last week?' she asked.

Harry looked away. 'Have I?'

She sighed. He still couldn't look her in the eye? Oh, this was bad. 'Yes, and we both know it. I thought we were friends.'

'We are.'

'So what's happening?' she asked.

He shrugged. 'I've no idea what you mean.'

'Then come round for a drink when you've finished your squash match.'

'Sorry, I can't. We're all going out for a pizza afterwards.'

She gave up. 'OK, have it your way. Clearly I'm making a massive fuss over nothing. Enjoy your squash match.'

Harry watched her walk away, feeling guilty. After all, she was right: he had been lying to her. He wasn't playing squash at all this evening, much less going out for a meal afterwards with friends.

He lasted another two hours before the guilt got the better of him and he texted her. Isla, are you at home?

It was a while before she replied. Why? I thought you were playing squash. League match, you said.

He squirmed, practically hearing the tones of Scottish disdain and knowing he deserved it. But she had been right earlier: they did need to clear the air. Is that offer of a drink still open?

For a nasty five minutes, he thought she was going to say no. And he'd deserve that, too.

Then his phone pinged. Sure.

Relief flooded through him. See you in an hour?

He stopped off at the supermarket and bought an armful of the nicest flowers he could find, a mix of sweet-smelling white and lilac stocks. By the time he stood on her doorstep after ringing the bell, he felt ridiculously nervous.

'For you,' he said, thrusting the flowers at her when she opened the door.

'Thank you—that's very kind of you. But what's the occasion?' she asked.

She deserved the truth. 'No occasion. It's guilt and an apology,' he said.

She looked puzzled. 'I'm not with you, but come in. Do you prefer red or white wine?'

'Whatever you've got open.'

'There's a bottle of pinot grigio in the fridge. Perhaps you'd like to open it for me while I put these gorgeous flowers in water,' she suggested. 'The glasses are in the cupboard above the kettle.'

He found the glasses and the wine, opened the bottle, and poured them both a drink while she arranged the flowers in a vase, then put the bottle back in the fridge. She ushered him through to the living room and he put the glasses down on the coffee table.

'So what's all this about, Harry?'

'You're right,' he said, 'about all of it. I *have* been avoiding you all week.'

'Why?'

He took a deep breath. 'Because we're supposed to be friends.'

She frowned. 'I thought we were.'

'We are.'

'Then...' Her frown deepened. 'Harry, you're not making any sense at all.'

'I know,' he said miserably. 'You were supposed to be safe.'

'And I'm not?'

'Far from it,' he said.

'Why?'

He sighed. 'Because I kissed you in Cornwall. Every time I see you, I want to do it again. And I know I'm rubbish at relationships and you've been hurt before, so the only thing I could do was stay out of your way,' he finished. 'Give me a few more days to get my head straight, and then hopefully I can look at you again without wanting to...' His mouth went dry as his imagination supplied the rest of it. Without wanting to pick her up, carry her to bed, and make love with her until they both saw stars.

'Without wanting to what, Harry?' she persisted.

'It doesn't matter,' he said, 'and I'm not going to make a nuisance of myself. But I thought you deserved an explanation and an apology.'

'Thank you.' She paused. 'But just supposing,' she asked softly, 'I've been thinking about Cornwall, too?'

'Then you're as crazy as I am,' he said, equally softly, 'because we can't do this. You've been badly hurt, and the last thing you need is to get mixed up with someone like me.'

'And how would you define someone like you?'

'You know what they call me at the hospital.' He shrugged. 'Harry the Heartbreaker. The man who won't date you more than three or four times because he doesn't do commitment.'

'That isn't the man I see,' she said. 'The man I see is kind, decent and caring. He notices the little things and he does his best to make everything right without making a huge song and dance about it all.'

'They're right about one thing. I don't do commitment,' he repeated. 'Come on, Isla. You've met my family.'

'And they're lovely.'

'They're lovely,' he agreed, 'but they're no good at commitment. My parents have ten marriages between them, including the one to each other. *Ten.* So it's in my genes to make a mess of things.'

'Or maybe,' she said, 'you could learn from your parents' mistakes.'

'I already have,' he said, 'and for me that means

not getting involved in a serious relationship.' He looked at the glass of wine he hadn't even touched. 'I'd better go.'

'Why?'

'You know why, Isla. Because I don't want to give in to temptation and do something that'll hurt us both.'

'You curled around me in your sleep,' she said.

Yeah. He knew. He'd woken with her in his arms, all warm and soft and sweet. It had taken every single bit of his strength to climb out of that bed instead of waking her with a kiss. 'So?' he asked, trying his best to drawl the word and sound totally uninterested.

'So,' she said, 'maybe I woke before you did and I didn't move away.'

'Seriously?' That had never occurred to him. And now she'd said it, he could hardly breathe.

'Seriously,' she said. 'And maybe I've been thinking about it every single morning since when I've woken up. And maybe the bed's felt way too big.'

He went very still. 'Are you saying...?' He

couldn't get the words out. Couldn't think straight. Was this really possible? Could they…?

'Maybe,' she said, 'I've been remembering how it felt when you kissed me.' She paused. 'And maybe I'd like you to do that again.'

'You'd actually risk a relationship with me?' he asked, wanting to make it clear.

'My head says no, that I should be sensible.'

'Fair enough.' He agreed with her completely.

'But there's another bit of me that thinks, maybe I shouldn't let what happened with Stewart wreck the rest of my life. Maybe it's time I was brave and took the risk.'

He could hardly breathe. She was choosing him? 'With me? But I'm about as high-risk as you could get.'

'I like you, Harry,' she said softly, 'and I think you like me, too. And I don't mean just as friends.'

'But what if it all goes wrong?' he asked. 'I can't promise you that this is going to work out. I can't promise you for ever.'

'I'm not expecting for ever. We're both adults. If it doesn't work out, then we'll be sensible about it and put our patients and the team first at work, just as we do now,' she said. 'But consider this, Harry—what if it goes right?'

His mouth went dry at the thought.

Risking a relationship with Isla McKenna.

Dating her.

Kissing her.

Making love with her.

He knew she'd been hurt. But if she was prepared to take the risk, then he'd have to step up to the plate and be brave, too.

'We need to set some ground rules,' he said.

She nodded. 'Ground rules sound fine to me.'

'Firstly, this is between you and me—as far as work is concerned, we're just colleagues.'

'That's sensible,' she said. 'Agreed.'

'Secondly, we're honest with each other—if we're uncomfortable with anything, then we say so.'

'Again, I don't have a problem with that.'

'Thirdly...' He couldn't think of anything else because his brain had turned to mush.

'Thirdly,' she said softly, 'why don't you just shut up and kiss me, Harry?'

Something he'd been aching to do ever since

Cornwall—ever since he'd first found out how sweet and soft her mouth was.

'That,' he said, 'is the best idea I've heard all day.' He took her hand and drew it to his lips.

He could feel the shiver run through her as he kissed the back of each finger in turn, keeping his gaze firmly fixed on hers. Yeah. Me, too, he thought. He ached with wanting her. He turned her hand over and brushed his mouth against her wrist, and she shivered again. Still keeping eye contact, he found her pulse point with his lips; he could feel it beating strong and hard.

And then he drew her into his arms and kissed her properly.

And it felt as if the sun had just come out and made everything shimmery and sparkling.

He ended up sitting on her sofa, with Isla on his lap, her head pillowed against his shoulder and their arms wrapped round each other.

'OK?' he asked softly.

'Very OK,' she said, stroked his face.

'I'm on an early shift tomorrow. You?'

'Same,' she said.

'Are you busy afterwards? Or can I see you?'

'I'm not busy. I'd like to see you,' she said.

'Dinner,' he said. 'And dress up. Because we're actually going to go on a proper date.'

She laughed. 'Why does that make me feel as if I'm eighteen years old again?'

'Me, too. Which is crazy.' He kissed her lightly. 'Right now I want to do all kinds of things, but I'm going to keep myself in check because I think we need to take this slowly. Get used to the idea.' He stole another kiss. 'I don't date. But for you I'm going to try to change. I don't know if I can,' he warned, 'but I'm going to try. That's the best I can promise.'

'And that's enough for me,' she said.

'Hmm.' He kissed her again. 'I'll see you at work tomorrow. And then I'll meet you here at seven.'

'Sounds perfect.' She wriggled off his lap, letting him stand up, then walked him to the door and stole a kiss. 'Good night, Harry. Sweet dreams.'

'They will be,' he said softly. 'You, too.'

Isla managed to concentrate on her patients for the whole of Saturday—it helped that she wasn't

Harry were rostered on different sections of the departments and their breaks didn't coincide—but anticipation prickled through her once she was back at her flat.

A proper date.

And he wanted her to dress up.

So it ought to be a little black dress.

She dug out her favourite dress from her wardrobe, and took time with her hair and make-up. Her efforts were rewarded when she opened the door to Harry and his eyes widened.

'You look stunning,' he said.

'Thank you. And so do you.' She'd seen him wearing a suit before, but she was so used to seeing him in a white coat at work that she'd forgotten how sexy he looked in formal dress.

He reached out to twirl the end of her hair round one forefinger. 'Your hair is glorious,' he said, his voice catching.

'Thank you.' She smiled. 'It gets in the way at work. That's why I wear it pinned back.'

'I like it both ways—when you're being a matron and when you're being a siren.'

She laughed. 'I'm not a matron—and I am so not starchy.'

'No, but you don't put up with any nonsense. Which is a good thing.'

'And I'm not a siren.'

'I beg to differ,' he said. 'You're the walking definition of sexy.'

She laughed again. 'Flatterer.'

'Nope. Statement of fact. And I can't wait to take you to dinner, Ms McKenna.' He glanced at her high heels. 'Can you walk in those?'

She rolled her eyes. 'I'm a nurse. I walk miles every day.'

'In flats.'

She took pity on him. 'Yes.'

'Good. Because it's a nice evening and I wanted to stroll hand in hand with you.'

'Works for me,' she said with a smile, and locked the door behind her.

They walked hand in hand to the tube station. Harry didn't say where they were going, but she also noted that he didn't have to stop and look up directions. Was it because he usually took his dates to wherever he'd booked a table, or did he just know London really well?

'This might be a bit cheesy,' he warned when they got to the West End. 'I've never been to this place before, but it's always on the list of the most romantic restaurants in London and the reviews are good. And I wanted to take you somewhere a bit special for our first date.'

So there she had her answers: he knew London well, and he'd never taken anyone else to this particular restaurant. Warmth spread through her and she found herself relaxing. And she fell in love with the restaurant on sight: the ceiling had been made into a canopy covered in white blossom and fairy lights, there were tealight candles on the tables casting a soft glow, the seats were all covered in red velvet, and the tablecloths were pure white damask.

'I can see exactly why this place tops the list,' she said. 'It's lovely.'

And the menu was equally good; she couldn't resist the hand-dived Scottish scallops, then corn-fed spring chicken with potato gnocchi, green beans and baby carrots. Harry joined her;

it tasted every bit as good as it sounded, and he insisted on sharing a bottle of champagne.

'This is fabulous,' she said, 'but remember we're going halves.'

'Absolutely not,' he told her, his dark eyes sincere. 'This is our first official date, so I am most definitely picking up the bill, but...'

Anticipation tightened in her stomach. Was he saying there were strings attached to dinner?

'If you want to buy me lunch tomorrow, I won't be offended,' he finished. 'Or just a chocolate brownie and some coffee in the hospital canteen, if you're working.'

'I'm off duty tomorrow. If you are, too, then it's a date for lunch,' she said.

'And a walk first,' he said. 'There's something I want to show you.'

'What?' she asked, intrigued.

'If I tell you now, it won't be a surprise tomorrow,' he said, tapping his nose and laughing.

She liked this side of Harry—the fun, charming, relaxed man.

And she enjoyed sharing a pudding with him,

even if he did eat more of the chocolate mille-feuille than she did.

'I've had a really lovely evening,' she said when he walked her back to her front door. 'Thank you.'

'My pleasure.'

'Do you want to come in?'

He stole a kiss. 'Yes. But I'm not going to. We're going to take this slowly.'

So neither of them would get afraid and back away? 'Works for me,' she said softly, and kissed him goodnight. 'I'll see you tomorrow.'

CHAPTER TEN

ON SUNDAY MORNING Harry woke, smiling, because he knew he was seeing Isla. He texted her to let her know he was on the way to meet her.

'So where are we going?' she asked when they left her flat.

'I thought we'd have a wander through the city.'

She smiled. 'Sounds good.'

When they emerged from the Tube station, Isla looked around and said, 'Isn't that Big Ben? So we're doing the touristy places?'

'Not especially,' he said, 'though if you want me to take a picture of you with Big Ben or the statue of Boudicca in the background, we can go up to the bridge.'

'No, I'm happy to go wherever you had in mind.'

He took her along the south bank, then groaned when they stopped. 'Sorry, I should've checked the tides.'

'Tides?' she asked.

'The Thames is a tidal river, so sometimes you see the beach just here and I thought you might like that. I guess it's the nearest you'll get to the sea in London.'

'Maybe another time,' she said.

They walked over the Millennium Bridge to St Paul's; then Harry led her through little side streets and a park to a part of Clerkenwell that was full of upscale clothes shops, jewellers, art shops and cafés.

'I thought we could have lunch here,' he said.

'This is lovely.' Most of the cafés had tables outside with umbrellas to shield their patrons from the sun; it made the place feel almost Mediterranean. 'Do you recommend anywhere in particular?' she asked.

'I haven't been here before,' Harry admitted. 'So pick one that takes your fancy.'

They browsed the menus on the boards outside; Isla chose a café with a French influence and they ordered a croque monsieur with freshly squeezed orange juice, then shared a brownie.

'Good choice,' Harry said. 'The food's great here.'

'And it's really nice exploring London with someone who actually knows the place,' Isla said.

'I've lived in London since I was eighteen. Obviously I don't know every single street, but I know a few nice out-of-the-way places,' he said, 'and it's always good to find somewhere new. I saw a write-up of this area in a magazine.' And he couldn't think of anyone he wanted to share this with more.

Funny, now he'd actually made the decision to start a proper relationship, it felt easy. Natural. The wariness he usually felt when dating someone had gone.

Or maybe it was because he'd found the right person.

Not that he was going to pressure Isla by telling her that. It was way too soon even to be thinking about it. They'd keep this low-key and fun, and see where it took them both.

At work, Harry and Isla managed to be professional with each other and treated each other strictly as colleagues. They were careful never to leave the hospital together unless it was as part of a group. Harry had persuaded Isla to open up a little more and come to one of the team nights out. He noticed that she thoroughly enjoyed the ten pin bowling, and went pink when one of the others told her they were all glad she'd come along because it was nice to get to know her outside work.

Later that evening, she told him, 'I'm glad you made me go. I really feel part of the team now.'

'Good. Welcome to London,' he said, and kissed her.

He saw Isla most days after work; one of them would cook, or they'd grab a takeaway, or if they'd gone into the city they'd find some nice little bistro. He felt they were getting closer, more and more in tune; the more he got to know her, the more he discovered they had in common. He actually felt in tune with her. There wasn't that antsy feeling that she'd expect more than he could give and it would all go spectacularly wrong. With her, he could relax and be himself—something he'd never experienced before. At the end of the evening it was getting harder to kiss her goodbye on her doorstep.

And it was harder to keep everything to himself at work, too. Whenever he saw Isla, it made him feel as if the sun had just come out. He found himself making excuses just so that their paths would cross in the department. And surely someone at the hospital would notice that he smiled more when she was around and start asking questions?

One Wednesday night when he'd walked her home after the cinema, she said to him, 'How brave are you feeling?'

'Why?' he asked.

'As we've made it way past your proverbial fourth date,' she said, 'I thought maybe we could, um, run a repeat of a certain garden in Cornwall. Except it won't be in a garden and we're not going to be interrupted. And this time we don't have to stop and be sensible.'

Heat rose through him. 'Are you saying…?'

'Yes.' She lifted her chin. 'I'm ready.'

The heat turned up a notch. 'Me, too,' he said softly. 'You have no idea how much I want you.'

'I think, Dr Gardiner, that might be mutual.' And the huskiness in her tone told him that she meant it.

Once she'd closed the front door behind them, he pulled her into his arms and kissed her. He nibbled her lower lip until she opened her mouth, letting him deepen the kiss. It was intoxicating; but it still wasn't enough. He needed the ultimate closeness.

He broke the kiss, whispering her name, and drew a trail of open-mouthed kisses all the way down her throat. She tipped her head back and gave a breathy little moan.

So she was as turned on as he was? Good— though he had no intention of stopping yet.

The thin strap of her top was no obstacle to him. He nuzzled along her shoulder, then along the line of her collarbones. 'I want you so much, Isla,' he whispered. 'Your skin's so soft, and I want to touch you. See you.'

'Do it,' she said, her voice shaky.

'Not here.' He picked her up.

'Troglodyte,' she teased.

'Yeah.' He stole another kiss. 'So where am I going?'

'Harry, my flat has four rooms and you've seen three of them. I hardly think you need directions or a map.'

He laughed. 'Sister McKenna, with her scathing Scottish common sense.' He carried her across the hallway to the one doorway he hadn't walked through. 'Are you sure about this, Isla?' he asked.

'Very sure.' She paused. 'Though do you have protection?'

'Yes.' He stole a kiss. 'And that's not because I'm taking you for granted or because I sleep around.'

'I know. You're being practical.'

'Exactly.' He wanted to make love with her but he didn't want to make a baby with her. He didn't want children. Ever. He'd already had that responsibility way too young in his life, and it had gone badly wrong. He wanted to keep life simple. *Safe*. None of that gut-wrenching fear.

He pushed the thoughts away, opened the door while balancing Isla in his arms, carried her over to the bed and then set her on her feet again. He let her slide down his body so she could feel how much she turned him on.

'Well, now, Dr Gardiner,' she said, but her voice was all breathy and her face was all pink and her eyes were all wide.

'Well, now, Sister McKenna,' he said, and his voice was as husky as hers. 'What next?'

'Your move,' she said.

'Good.' He slid his fingers under the hem of her top, stroked along the flat planes of her abdomen. 'May I?' he asked softly.

She nodded, and let him peel the soft jersey material over her head.

She was wearing a strapless bra; he traced the edges of the material with his fingertips, then slid one hand behind her back, stroked along her spine and unhooked her bra.

'You're beautiful,' he whispered as the garment fell to the floor.

Colour heated her face. 'And I feel very overdressed.'

'Your move,' he said.

She was almost shy in the way she undid his

shirt and slid the soft cotton off his shoulders. 'Very nice pectorals, Dr Gardiner.' She smiled and slid her hands across his chest, then down over his abdomen. 'And that's a proper six-pack.'

'So we're touching as well as looking now, are we?' He cupped her breasts and rubbed the pad of his thumbs across her hardening nipples.

She shivered. 'Oh, yes, we're touching.'

'Touching isn't enough. I want to taste you, Isla. Explore you.' He dropped to his knees and took one nipple into his mouth. She slid her hands into his hair; he could feel the slight tremor in her hands as he teased her with his lips and his tongue.

She followed his lead, dropping to her knees and undoing the button of his jeans.

He did the same with hers, then leaned his forehead against her bare shoulder and chuckled.

'What's so funny?' she asked.

'We didn't think this through.' He gestured to their positions. 'Right now I'll be able to pull your jeans down as far as your knees, and that's about it.'

She looked at him. 'And we're on the floor,

when there's a nice soft bed right next to us. How old are we, sixteen?'

He stole a kiss. 'You make me feel like a teenager. In a good way, though; there's none of the angst and fear that the first time's going to be a disaster instead of perfect.' He nibbled her earlobe. 'Because we're both old enough to know it's not going to be perfect or a disaster.'

'What is it going to be, then?' she asked.

'An exploration. Discovering what each other likes. Where and how we like to be touched. Kissed.' He punctuated his words with kisses, then got to his feet, took her hands and drew her to her feet beside him.

'Starting here,' he said, and finished undoing her jeans. He stooped to slide the denim down over her curves and helped her step out of them. 'Your move, I think.'

She did the same with him, then grinned. 'You're wearing odd socks.'

'It's a London thing. A trend. The ultimate in sophistication,' he said.

She laughed. 'Is it, hell.'

'Busted.' He kissed her. 'I wasn't paying attention last time I did my laundry. I was thinking of you. Fantasising.'

'Oh, yes?'

'Definitely yes.'

He got rid of the rest of their clothes, pushed the duvet to one side, then picked her up and laid her against the pillows. 'You look like a mermaid,' he said, kneeling down beside her.

'A mermaid?'

'With that glorious hair spread out like that—definitely a mermaid. Or maybe a Victorian model for some super-sultry goddess,' he mused.

'Compliment accepted.' She reached up to stroke his face. 'And you're as beautiful as a Michelangelo statue.'

'Why, thank you.' He leaned forward to steal a kiss. 'And your skin's like alabaster, except you're warm and you smell of peaches.'

He nuzzled his way down her sternum, then paid attention to the soft underside of her breasts. 'You're incredibly lovely,' he said.

'Just like you fantasised when you were doing your laundry?'

'Way better,' he said. He rocked back on his haunches. 'I want to explore you,' he said softly.

Colour bloomed again in her cheeks. 'I'm all yours.'

He started at the hollows of her anklebones, stroking and kissing his way up to the back of her knees. Her breathing had grown shallow by the time he parted her thighs, and she slid her hands into his hair to urge him on. She shivered when he drew his tongue along her sex, dragged in a breathy moan when he did it again, and when he started teasing her clitoris he heard her murmured 'oh' of pleasure.

Harry was really looking forward to watching Isla fall apart under his touch. He loved the idea that he could turn all that sharp common sense to mush, just for a little while.

Her body tensed, and he felt the moment that her climax hit.

'Harry,' she whispered, and he shifted up the bed so he could hold her tightly.

'OK?' he asked when she'd stopped shaking.

'Very OK—I wasn't expecting that,' she said. 'I thought you said this wasn't going to be perfect?'

He smiled and stroked her face. 'I'm not finished yet, not by a long way.'

'No—I think it's my turn to make you fall apart,' she said. Her hands were warm and sure as she explored him.

Harry loved the way she made him feel, the way his blood heated with desire as she stroked and caressed him. Then she dipped her head so that glorious hair brushed against his skin, and desire surged through him.

'Isla,' he said softly, 'I love what you're doing to me and you feel like heaven—but right now I really, *really* need to be inside you.'

'Your wish is my command,' she teased. 'Condom?'

'In my wallet—in my jeans pocket.'

She climbed off the bed, fished his wallet out of his jeans and threw it to him. He caught it and took out the condom. 'Are you really sure about this?'

'Really sure,' she said, her voice husky, and took the little foil packet from him. She opened it, rolled it over his shaft and leaned over him to kiss him. 'Do you have any idea how sexy you look, lying there on my bed?'

'Not as sexy as you'll look with your hair spread over the pillow like a mermaid,' he replied.

'Hmm, so the man has a thing about mermaids?'

He drew her down to him, shifted so that she was lying beneath him and knelt between her thighs. 'Yeah,' he said, and eased into her.

It was very far from the first time that he'd ever made love, but it was the first time that Harry had ever felt this kind of completeness, this kind of bond.

Which made Isla McKenna dangerous to his peace of mind.

But she drew him so much that he couldn't resist her. Didn't want to resist her.

She held him tightly as his climax burst through him.

CHAPTER ELEVEN

WHEN HARRY HAD floated back to earth, he moved carefully. 'Help yourself to anything you need in the bathroom,' Isla said. 'The linen cupboard's in there with fresh towels.'

'Thanks.'

Isla lay curled in bed while Harry was in the bathroom, feeling warm and comfortable and that all was right with the world. She didn't bother getting up and dressing; Harry hadn't taken his clothes with him to the bathroom, and she was pretty sure that he'd come back to bed with her. Like Cornwall all over again, except this time they wouldn't be falling asleep on opposite sides of the bed, trying to keep a careful distance between them. This time, they'd fall asleep in each other's arms.

When Harry came back, his skin was still damp from the shower and he looked utterly gorgeous.

'I'm afraid I smell of flowers,' he said. 'Your shower gel's a bit, um, girly.'

She laughed. 'Actually, in Regency times, there was very little difference between the scents men and women used. Lots of them were floral—based on rose, lavender or orange flower water.'

He looked intrigued. 'How do you know that?'

'I read a lot of Regency romances,' she said, 'and I was interested in all the social history side of things. I looked up a few things on the Internet—according to one of the really long-established London perfume houses, Beau Brummell's favourite scent involved lavender.'

'Beau Brummell? Hmm. So you like Regency dandies, do you?'

'And Scottish lairds—and I dare you to say it's girly for a man to wear a kilt.'

He laughed. 'Can you imagine me in a kilt?'

'Oh yes—especially if you let your hair grow a bit.'

'My hair?'

'You know your mermaid thing? Well, that's me and period drama. It's the sort of thing I love watching on telly. And you'd be the perfect period drama hero,' she said. 'I can imagine you riding horseback and wearing a tricorn hat.'

'We could always play the lady and the highwayman,' he said with a grin. 'I think I'd like that. Hands up, my lady.'

'Now, you need a domino mask to do that properly, and maybe a white silk scarf over your face, otherwise I could tell the local magistrate what you look like and you'd get arrested.' She laughed. 'Come back to bed.'

He shook his head. 'Sorry, I really need to go. I'm on an early shift tomorrow.'

'I have an alarm clock.'

'Even so. I don't have a change of clothes or a toothbrush.'

'I can always put your stuff through the washing machine, and I'm pretty sure I have a spare toothbrush in the bathroom cabinet.'

But he wouldn't be swayed. And the carefree, laughing man who'd just teased her about her highwayman fantasy had suddenly gone distant on her.

He got dressed in about ten seconds flat.

And Isla felt wrong-footed, unsure what to do

next. Should she get dressed and see him out? Or just grab her dressing gown?

But when she moved to get out of bed, he said, 'Stay there. You look comfortable. I'll see myself out.'

'OK.'

'See you tomorrow,' he said.

'Sure,' she said, masking the flood of hurt that he could walk away so easily. And she noticed that he didn't even kiss her goodbye before he left. How could he switch from being so sexy and dishevelled to so cool and dispassionate, so very fast?

She'd thought they were both ready for the next step, but had this been an intimacy too far? Was Harry having second thoughts about their relationship? And would he revert to being the heartbreaker that the hospital grapevine said he was? Was he right when he said he wasn't capable of committing to a relationship?

Bottom line: had she just made a really, really stupid mistake?

The questions went round and round in her head. And she had no answers at all.

* * *

Harry knew he'd behaved badly.

He'd seen the hurt in Isla's face, even though she'd masked it quickly.

And he'd bet right now that she was feeling used. That he'd basically had his way with her and walked away.

Ah, hell.

This was a mess.

Maybe he needed to be honest with her and tell her that he was running scared. Panicking. But that would mean admitting that his feelings about her were changing. That he thought he might be falling in love with her—her warmth, shot through with common sense and humour that he found irresistible.

He didn't get involved. He'd never wanted to get involved. He'd seen the carnage it left behind every time his parents divorced their current partner—and, even though everyone eventually managed to be civil for the children's sake, he knew from first-hand experience what it felt like in the early days. When your world crumbled round you and you thought it was your fault, that you'd done something bad that made it impossible for your parents to live together. When you didn't understand what was going on.

And so he'd always kept his relationships light. Walked away before things started getting serious.

Except this time it was too late. It was already serious between him and Isla. And he didn't know when or how that had happened. They'd started off as friends; then, little by little, he'd fallen in love with her. Everything from her dry, slightly scathing sense of humour through to the way she smiled. From the cool, capable way she handled every crisis at work through to her sensual delight in eating out.

The blood seemed to rush out of his head as it hit home: he was in love with her.

Which left him stuck between a rock and a hard place.

Either he walked away from Isla—which would hurt; or he let their relationship move forward, risking being hurt even more when it went wrong. Because it *would* go wrong: he'd learned that from his parents. Love didn't last.

Isla had said at his father's wedding that she thought he had the capacity to make a relationship work—that he was isolating himself, and it was wrong because he was loyal and kind and loving.

But he wasn't so sure. Did he really have that capacity?

He'd already hurt her. Guilt prickled at him. He knew she'd wanted him to stay, and yet he'd walked away. Rejected her. Let his own fears get in the way. He hadn't been fair to her. At all.

And he slept badly enough that night that he texted her first thing in the morning.

I'm sorry. I was an idiot last night.

Her reply was suitably crisp: Yes, you were.

I don't have any excuses.

But he wasn't quite ready to admit the truth—that he'd never felt like this about anyone before and it left him in a flat spin.

But can you forgive me?

It was a big ask, and he knew it.

I'll think about it, she replied. See you at work.

Would things have changed between them at work? It was the one constant in his life, the place where he was sure of himself and knew he belonged. He didn't want that to change. And he was antsy all the way to the hospital.

But Sister McKenna was as calm and professional as she always was, treating Harry just like she treated every other member of the team. It helped that they weren't rostered on together; and Harry was able to relax and sort out his patients' problems.

Isla didn't reply to his text suggesting dinner. She also hadn't said anything about any other arrangements, so he bought flowers and chocolates and headed over to her flat. If she wasn't in, then he'd leave his apology with a neighbour.

Thankfully, she was in.

And she frowned when she saw the flowers and chocolates. 'Harry, what is this?'

'An apology,' he said.

She raised an eyebrow. 'Would you be repeating your father's mistakes, by any chance?'

It had never occurred to him before: but, yes, he was. Now he thought about it, Bertie was always sending flowers or chocolates to apologise for behaving badly. 'Ah,' he said, and grimaced. 'I think the penny might just have dropped.'

'I don't want you to give me flowers or chocolates when we fall out,' she said.

No. He knew that she wanted something that would cost him far more. She wanted him to talk to her. To open his heart.

He blew out a breath. 'I'm really not good at this sort of stuff, Isla.'

'Would a mug of tea help?'

Even though he knew it had strings attached, he nodded. Because he knew she was making more of a concession than he deserved.

'Come in. And thank you for the flowers. Though if you ever buy me flowers again,' she warned, 'then I might hit you over the head with them.'

'Noted. Though I guess at least they'd be soft,' he said, trying for humour.

To his relief, she laughed.

Taking heart from her reaction, he walked forward and put his arms round her. 'I'm sorry. It's just...'

'You don't do relationships, and I asked you to stay the night. Which is tantamount to proposing to you with a megaphone while standing on a table in the middle of the hospital canteen.'

'In a nutshell,' he agreed. 'Isla—I did warn you I was rubbish at relationships.'

'And you're using your parents as an excuse,' she said.

He winced. 'You don't pull your punches.'

'You're the one who set the ground rules,' she reminded him. 'Honesty.'

'You want honesty?' He leaned his forehead against hers. 'OK. I want to be with you. I want to make a go of this. The way I feel... I...' He blew out a breath. 'I'm never this inarticulate. Sorry. I'm making a mess of this. But I don't want to hurt you, and I don't want to end up hurt either.'

'Then you need to make a leap of faith. Is it really so hard to stay the night?'

'Last time I did that...' His voice faded. 'Actually, the last time I spent the night with anyone was with you. But the time before that—my girlfriend assumed that our relationship meant more to me than it did. And it got messy.'

'Spending the night,' she said, 'means both of us get a little more sleep before work, the next day. But I guess you didn't bring a change of clothes or a toothbrush.'

'No. Can you be a little bit patient with me?' he asked.

'I can, but there's a string attached.'

He wasn't sure he wanted to know the answer, but he knew he had to ask the question. 'Which is?'

'As long as you promise to talk to me in future,' she said.

He remembered something that gave him a way out. 'I thought you liked brooding Regency rakes?'

'In period dramas on screen or in books, yes,' she said. 'In real life, they'd be a pain in the neck. I'd rather have openness and the truth, even if it hurts.' She gave him a wry smile. 'Because the alternative is leaving me to guess what's in your head. And I'm not a mind-reader. What I imagine can hurt me far more than the truth.'

'I'm sorry,' he said. 'I…have feelings for you.' There, it was out. The best he could say for now, anyway. He wasn't ready to say the L-word; he was still trying to come to terms with his feelings.

Odd. At work, he could always find the right words. Here, when it really mattered, he found himself silent. He couldn't even quote a song or poetry at her. His mind had gone completely blank. He felt numb and stupid and awkward.

She stroked his face. 'I have feelings for you, too, Harry. One of them's exasperation.'

He knew he deserved it. But he took a tiny risk and stole a kiss. 'I'm trying, Isla. This isn't easy for me.'

'I know.' She kissed him back. 'But we'll get there. We'll just have to work on it a bit harder. Together.'

She had more faith in him that than he did, he thought wryly.

Harry still hadn't quite managed to spend the whole night with Isla when she went back to the Western Isles to see her family for four days, the week before her birthday. She didn't ask him to go with her, and he wasn't sure if he was more relieved or disappointed.

He was shocked to discover just how much he missed her during those four days. Even though there was a team night out and a squash match to keep him busy on two of those evenings, he still missed her. The odd text and snatched phone call just weren't enough.

And if he put it all together, it was obvious. He was ready to move on. To take the next step. To take a risk. With her.

Surreptitiously, he checked out her off-duty for the week of her birthday and changed his own off-duty to match. He didn't want to take the next step in London; it would be better on neutral ground. If he took her away for her birthday, he'd be able to relax instead of panicking that it was all going to go wrong. He spent the evening researching, and found what he hoped would be the perfect place.

He knew which flight she was catching back to London, and met her at the airport with an armful of flowers.

'They're soft ones,' he said, 'because I remember what you said you'd do next time I bought you flowers.' Hit him over the head with them.

She laughed, clearly remembering. 'I meant if you gave me apology flowers instead of talking things through,' she said. 'These are different. They're romantic. Welcome-home flowers. I love them.'

He knew she wanted the words. And he was half-surprised that he was ready to say them. 'I missed you,' he said. 'A lot.'

'I missed you, too.'

'Did you have a good time?'

She nodded. 'It was lovely. It made me realise how much I miss the island. The sky and the mountains and the freshness of the air. And most of all, the sea.'

Then there was a fair chance that she'd really love what he'd arranged for her birthday. Though a nasty thought struck him. If she was homesick... 'Do you miss it enough to want to go back?'

'I've moved on,' she said softly, 'and they re-

placed me at the practice, so if I went back now...'
She shrugged. 'I wouldn't have a place, really.'

'But you've retrained. You're an emergency
nurse. I assume there are hospitals on the islands?'

'I could work in the emergency department
in Benbecula, or in the GP acute department in
Stornoway,' she said.

'But?'

She shook her head. 'Not right now. Maybe
some time in the future.'

So she did want to go back. Then what was
stopping her? He remembered what she'd told
him about the way people had behaved towards
her after the whole thing blew up with her fiancé's stepfather. 'Are people still giving you a hard
time about Gillespie?'

'No, but I did see Stewart while I was there.'

He went cold. That night after their fight and
he'd admitted to his feelings... She'd said she had
feelings for him, too. But had seeing her ex again
changed that? Maybe the surprise he'd planned
for her birthday was a bad idea after all.

'He's engaged to another lass,' she said, 'someone we both went to school with, and I wish them both well.'

'And you're OK about that?' he asked softly.

She nodded. 'I've moved on. I've met someone else. Someone I really like.'

He smiled and kissed her. 'I like you, too.' More than liked, if he was honest about it, but he wasn't quite ready to say it yet. 'So it's your birthday on Monday.'

'Yes. I assume it's standard practice to bring in cake for everyone in the department?'

'And chocolate bars for those off duty,' he confirmed. 'And birthdays are always celebrated at the local pizza place with the team, so I'm afraid I can't take you out to dinner on your actual birthday.'

'Because otherwise people will work it out that we're an item.'

He knew that hurt her, but he still wasn't quite ready to go public. 'However,' he said, 'you're off duty two days later—that's when I'm taking you out to dinner.' He paused. 'And you'll need to pack.'

'Pack?' She looked surprised, then wary.

Did she think that he was asking her to stay at his place? 'For two days,' he said. 'It's part of your birthday present. You'll need casual stuff for walking, and something nice to dress up in. I'll pick you up at your place after your shift.'

It was good to be back in London. Isla had a feeling that Harry had missed her as much as she'd missed him—his lovemaking that evening was even more tender—but she noticed that he still didn't stay overnight.

Though he was planning to take her away for her birthday, the following week. But then a nasty thought struck her: were they sharing a room, or had he booked separate rooms?

On her birthday, she was touched to discover that banners and balloons had been put up in the staffroom, and the team had clubbed together to buy her some gorgeous earrings. She thoroughly enjoyed the team night out at the pizza place, especially as someone had arranged for a birthday cake with candles and everyone sang 'Happy birthday' to her.

Harry saw her home afterwards, and gave her

a beautifully wrapped parcel. 'It's the first bit of your present,' he said. It was a beautiful bangle, inlaid with precious stones, and he'd clearly paid attention to the kind of things she liked. But again, he didn't stay the night. Not even on her birthday. And it hurt. Would he ever be ready to spend the night with her—to make a move towards a greater commitment?

Isla was rushed off her feet on the early shift on the Tuesday. Harry still hadn't told her where they were going, but after their shift he picked her up in his little red sports car and drove her down to the Dorset coast, down a tiny track to a lighthouse.

'We're staying here?' she asked, surprised. 'That's just lovely.'

'For two nights,' he said. 'I know you miss the sea and I thought you'd like it here.'

It was incredibly romantic; there was a four-poster bed against one wall, opposite picture windows that overlooking the sea. She walked over to the window and gazed out. 'Harry, this is so perfect. Thank you.'

And he'd booked only one room. She knew that

for him spending the whole night together was a huge turning point. For the first time, she really started to hope that he could get past his fear of falling in love and they had a future.

'I got it right, then?' For a moment, he looked really vulnerable.

'More than right,' she said, kissing him. 'However did you find this place?'

'Just did a bit of research,' he said. 'Luckily, because it's midweek, they had a vacancy.'

Dinner was fabulous: locally caught fish, followed by local ice cream on Dorset apple cake. But better still was afterwards, when Harry carried her over the threshold to the four-poster bed. It felt almost like a honeymoon, Isla thought.

In the next morning, she woke in his arms. And, unlike their trip to Cornwall, Harry made love with her before breakfast.

The morning was bright; they went to Lyme Regis and walked along the famous harbour wall of the Cobb, then headed for the cliffs and looked among the loose stones for fossils. Harry was the first one to find an ammonite and presented it to Isla with a bow. Then they headed for the boulders; they were marvelling over the massive ammonites embedded in the rock bed when they heard a scream from the shallows.

A small girl was holding her foot up and crying, while her mother was clearly trying to calm her down and find out what had just happened.

'Maybe the poor kid's trodden on something sharp,' Harry suggested.

'Do you think we ought to go and offer to help?' Isla asked.

'Yes,' Harry said, and took her hand.

'We're medics,' he said to the little girl's mum, who was sitting on the sand next to her daughter, looking at the little girl's foot. 'Can we help?'

'Abbie said she trod on something and it hurt— I can't see anything but I wondered if she'd trodden on some glass,' the mum said.

'Abbie, I'm Dr Harry,' he said to the little girl, 'and this is Nurse Isla. Can we look at your foot?'

The little girl was still crying, but nodded shyly.

'I can't see any glass or any blood like you'd get with a cut,' Harry said, 'but I think she might have stood on a weever fish. They bury themselves in the sand under shallow water; the spines on their back and gills are laced with venom, and it feels like a sting if you step on them.' He showed the woman the swollen and reddening spot on Abbie's foot. 'We'd better get her over to the lifeguards' hut. We need some tweezers so we can take the spine out, clean the area with soap and water and rinse it with fresh water, then put Abbie's foot in hot water so it'll "cook" the protein in the venom and stop it hurting. And hopefully they'll have some infant paracetamol.'

'I've got the paracetamol,' Abbie's mum said.

'Good. I'll carry her over for you,' he said.

'I'll go ahead and talk to them so they can put the kettle on and get the first aid kit out,' Isla said.

Harry carried Abbie to the hut where the lifeguards were working. Isla had already explained their theory, and the first aid kit was out already.

He set Abbie gently on the bed so he could crouch down and examine her foot again, this time with a torch illuminating the area. 'I can get one of the spines out, but there's another one near the joint of her big toe, so I'd like that one looked at in the nearest emergency department,' he said.

One of the lifeguards called the ambulance while Harry took out the weever fish spine he could see easily, and the other provided a deep bowl of hot water.

'Ow, it's hot!' Abbie said, crying again.

'I know, sweetheart, but you need to put your foot in to stop it hurting,' Harry said. 'If you can do that for me, I'll tell you a story.'

'All right,' Abbie said bravely.

He'd just finished telling her a long-drawn-out version of the Three Little Pigs—where he had everyone in the lifeguards' hut booming out the wolf's threat to huff and puff and blow the house down—when the ambulance arrived. Harry gave a quick rundown to the paramedics.

'Thank you so much for looking after us,' Abbie's mum said. 'And I'm so sorry we took up your time on your holiday.'

'It's fine,' he said with a smile. 'Hope Abbie feels better soon.'

He was so good with children, Isla thought. So why was he so adamant he didn't want children of his own? What had happened in his past? Had he dated someone with a child and it had all gone wrong? But she couldn't think of a way to ask him without it seeming like prying. She'd have to wait until he was ready to open up to her and talk about it. But Harry was stubborn. Would he ever be ready?

'Well, Dr Gardiner, I think you earned a pot of tea and a scone with jam and clotted cream,' she said lightly.

'Sounds good to me,' Harry said, and looped his arm round her shoulders.

They ended up spending the rest of the day at the coast, eating fish and chips on the cliff-top and watching the setting sun. The spectacular flares of red and orange faded to yellow at the horizon, and the colours were reflected across the sea.

'Definitely a selfie moment,' Harry said, and took a picture of them on his phone with the sunset behind them.

This was perfect, Isla thought. It couldn't have been a nicer day.

The next day, they went exploring again; they stopped to walk up the hill and view the famous natural limestone arch of Durdle Door, and discovered the enormous chalk-cut figure of the Cerne Giant looming across another hill. And just being together was so good.

Back in London, this time Harry stayed overnight at Isla's flat.

They'd definitely taken a step forward, she thought. And maybe, just maybe, this was going to work out.

CHAPTER TWELVE

OVER THE NEXT couple of months, Harry and Isla grew closer still. They both kept a change of clothes and toiletries at each other's flat, though they were careful not to arrive at work together when they were on the same shift, and they hadn't made a big deal of letting people know that they were an item.

But one morning Isla felt really rough when she got out of bed.

'Are you all right?' Harry asked.

'I feel a bit queasy,' Isla admitted. 'I think maybe I'm coming down with that bug that's hit the department.' Which probably explained why she seemed to have gone off coffee, the last few days.

'Maybe you ought to stay home and call in sick,' Harry said. 'If you've got the lurgy, you don't want to spread it to the rest of the team or the patients.'

Normally it took a lot more than a bug to stop Isla working her shift, but right at that moment she felt absolutely terrible. 'Yes, I think you're right,' she said.

Harry made her some toast and a mug of hot lemon and honey; he also brought a jug of iced water in to the bedroom and put it by her bedside. 'Can I get you anything else to make you comfortable? A book or a magazine?'

'I'll be fine. But thank you.' She smiled. 'You have a lovely bedside manner. Anyone would think you were a doctor.'

'Yeah, yeah.' He grinned back. 'Text me later to let me know how you're feeling, OK?'

'Yes—though I was thinking, maybe you'd better not come back here after work today. I don't want you to pick it up.'

'I've got the constitution of an ox,' he claimed. 'Look, I'll call you when I leave work and see how you're doing, and then you can tell me if you want me to pick up anything from the shops for you.' He kissed her forehead. 'For now, get some rest.'

Isla lay curled up in bed with a magazine for

the rest of the morning. She was feeling considerably better by lunchtime, and she felt a bit guilty about being off sick when she was clearly fine. Or maybe she'd been lucky and had the super-mild version of the bug and it was over now. She texted Harry to say she felt better and was just going out to get a bit of fresh air. But, when she went to the corner shop to buy some milk, the woman in the queue in front of Isla was wearing some really strong perfume which made her feel queasy again; and the smell of greasy food wafting from the fast food place next door to the corner shop made her feel even worse.

When she got back home, it slammed into her. Nausea first thing, a heightened sense of smell, an aversion to coffee... If a patient had described those symptoms to her, she would've suggested doing a pregnancy test. But she couldn't be pregnant—could she?

They'd always been really careful to use condoms.

Although, the night of her birthday, they'd got carried away with the sheer romance of having a bedroom in a lighthouse, and maybe that night they hadn't been as careful then as they should've been.

She thought back. Her last period had been really light, and she knew that women sometimes had breakthrough bleeding during early pregnancy. Could she be pregnant?

It niggled at her for the next hour.

In the end, she went to the local supermarket and picked up a pregnancy test. This would prove once and for all that she was making a fuss about nothing.

She did the test and stared at the little window, willing the words 'not pregnant' to appear. Although she hoped that Harry was revising his views on the 'never settling down' question, she was pretty sure that his stance on never having children of his own hadn't changed. She knew he was dead set against it.

She kept staring at the window. Then, to her horror, the word 'pregnant' appeared. Followed by '3+'—meaning that she was more than three weeks pregnant.

What?

She couldn't be.

Maybe the test was faulty. Maybe there was a problem with the pixels or something in the area on the screen that should've said 'not', and that was why it was blank. Just as well there were two kits in the box.

She did the second one, just to reassure herself that the first one was a mistake.

Except the result was the same: Pregnant. More than three weeks.

Oh, no. She was going to have to tell Harry.

But how? How, when she knew that he didn't want children? When he was practically phobic about it?

She still hadn't found the words by the time he called her.

'I've just finished my shift now, so I'm on my way to see you,' he said. 'Do you want me to pick up anything from the shops?'

'No, thanks—it's fine.'

'How are you feeling?' he asked.

Panicky. 'Better,' she lied. 'But I think maybe it'd be best if you didn't come over, just in case I'm still incubating this bug.'

And that would give her time to work out how to tell him the news, wouldn't it?

Except she still hadn't come up with anything by the next morning. She felt even queasier than she had the previous morning and only just made it to the bathroom before she was sick.

Grimly, she washed her face and cleaned her teeth.

She definitely couldn't let Harry stay over— or stay with him—until she'd told him the news, because she didn't want him to work it out for himself. Which of course he would, if she dashed out of bed and threw up every morning.

She just hoped that none of her patients that day would be wearing particularly strong perfume or aftershave, and that she could either avoid the hospital canteen completely or they'd have totally bland foods on the menu with no smell.

Thankfully, she wasn't rostered on with Harry. But he caught up with her at her break. 'Are you sure you should be in? How are you feeling?' he asked, his dark eyes filled with concern.

'Fine,' she fibbed, and sipped her glass of water

in the hope that it would stop her reacting to the smell of his coffee. 'How was your morning?'

'Rushed off my feet.' He grimaced. 'I had one mum bringing in a sick baby, but she had two more children with her under school age, both of them with rotten colds. Clearly she hadn't been able to get anyone to babysit them while she brought the baby in to us. It was total chaos, with both of the toddlers wanting their mum's attention, and she was trying to explain the baby's symptoms to me at the same time. I couldn't hear myself think.'

'Was the baby OK?'

'She had bronchiolitis,' he said. 'Classic intercostal recession. I sent her up to the children's ward. I took a sample of mucus from her nose, but I'm pretty sure it'll be RSV positive. It's the beginning of the RSV season,' he said with a sigh, 'where they'll have two bays of the children's ward full of babies on oxygen therapy, and every single member of staff up there will have the cold from hell.' He rolled his eyes. 'And people wonder why I never want to have kids.'

She flinched inwardly, knowing that he was

just exaggerating a bit to make his morning sound dramatic—or was he? He was always brilliant with any sick children who came into the department, and at the wedding he'd been so good with his youngest brother. Yet he'd always been adamant that he didn't want kids of his own and he'd never really explained why. When she'd tried to ask him, he'd simply changed the subject.

So she really wasn't looking forward to telling him the news that, actually, he was going to be a dad. She had to find a way to soften the blow for him, but she had no idea how.

'Do you want to come over for dinner tonight?' he asked.

'I'm still feeling a bit fragile, so I think I'd better pass and have an early night with a hot water bottle,' she said. She knew she was being a coward, but she really needed to work out the right way to tell him. A way that wouldn't hurt him. Just… How?

Was it his imagination, Harry wondered a couple of days later, or was Isla trying to avoid him? Ever since she'd gone down with that bug, she'd been acting strangely. Had she changed her mind about their relationship? He'd been seriously thinking about it himself; he'd never felt like this about anyone else before in his life. And she made him feel that the world was a better place. Just being with her made his heart feel lighter. He'd started to think about asking her to move in with him, maybe even take the next step and get engaged. Take the risk he'd always avoided in the past, so sure it would go wrong because he'd seen it go wrong so often for both his parents.

But now Isla seemed to be going distant on him, he was having doubts about it again. Did he have it all wrong? Did she not feel the same as he did, any more? Or was he so messed up about the idea of commitment that he couldn't see straight?

By the end of the week he was really concerned. They hadn't spent any time together for more than a week, so something was definitely wrong. All he could do was persuade Isla to go somewhere quiet with him, and then maybe he could talk to her and find out what the problem was. And then he could solve it. He hoped.

They had a busy shift in Resus that morning, and Harry was about to suggest that they went for a break between patients when the paramedics brought in in a woman who'd been in an RTA.

'Mrs Paulette Freeman,' the paramedic said. 'A bicycle courier cut in front of her; she had to swerve to avoid him, and crashed into the car on her right-hand side, which made her air bag go off. She's thirty years old, and twelve weeks pregnant with her first baby. There haven't been any problems so far in the pregnancy, and when we examined her there was no sign of bleeding. Her blood group is A positive.'

Harry and Isla exchanged a glance of relief at the news about the blood group. At least there wouldn't be a risk to the fetus from rhesus antibodies.

'Can you remember, did you bang your head at all, Mrs Freeman?' Harry asked.

'No, but the airbag went straight into my stomach.' Mrs Freeman looked anxious. 'Is my baby all right? Maybe I shouldn't have worn my seat belt.'

'Seat belts really do reduce the risk of serious

injury in pregnancy,' Harry reassured her, 'so you did the right thing. Now, I'm going to examine you—just let me know if any area feels a bit tender.'

'My stomach's a bit sore,' she said, 'but that's probably from the airbag. It doesn't matter about me. What about the baby?'

'The baby's pretty well cushioned in there but of course you're worried. My job now is to see how you both are,' Harry said. 'Try and relax for me.' He added quietly to Isla, 'Call the maternity department and get Theo Petrakis down here, please. I always play it super-safe with pregnant patients.' He turned back to Mrs Freeman. 'Is there someone we can call for you?'

'My husband,' she said.

'I'll do that. Can you tell me his number?' Isla asked, then wrote the number down as Mrs Freeman said it. 'I'll call him straight away and ask him to come in,' she said.

'I'm going to examine your stomach now, Mrs Freeman,' Harry said. 'Tell me if anything hurts.'

She was white-faced and tight-lipped, and didn't say a word. He couldn't feel any uterine contractions, but the uterus felt firmer than he'd like.

A pelvic examination showed no sign of bleeding, which he hoped was a good thing. But he was starting to get a bad feeling about this case.

'I'm just going to listen to the baby's heartbeat,' he said, and set up the Doppler probe. But instead of the nice fast clop-clop he was expecting to hear, there was silence. He couldn't pick up the baby's heartbeat.

'What's wrong?' Mrs Freeman asked. 'Why can't we hear the baby's heartbeat?'

'I'm sure there's nothing to worry about,' Harry reassured her. 'Often this particular machine doesn't work very well in the first trimester. I'll try the old-fashioned way—obviously you won't be able to hear it, but I will.' He picked up a horn-shaped Pinard stethoscope; but, to his dismay, he still couldn't hear anything.

Isla came back in. 'I've spoken to your husband, Mrs Freeman, and he's on his way in. Dr Gardiner, Mr Petrakis is on his way down right now.'

'Good. I just want to get the portable ultrasound. I'll be back in a tick,' Harry said, doing his best to sound calm and breezy.

Isla had clearly seen the Doppler and the Pinard next to the bed and obviously worked out that he hadn't been able to pick up the baby's heartbeat, because when he brought the machine back she was sitting next to the bed, holding Mrs Freeman's hand.

Harry's bad feeling suddenly got a whole lot worse.

He knew that pregnant women could lose a lot of blood before they started showing any sign of hypovolaemic shock. In a case like this, with blunt force trauma, there was a high risk of placental abruption—where the placenta separated from the uterus before the baby was born—and the fetus was likely to suffer. Worst-case scenario, the baby wouldn't survive. Although there was no sign of bleeding, with a concealed placental abruption the blood remained in the uterus. It was the more severe form of abruption and if his fears were correct the baby had already died.

'I'm going to do an ultrasound now to see what's going on,' he said. 'It's very like the machine they used when they did your dating scan, Mrs Freeman. Can you bare your stomach again for me so I can put some gel on it? I'm afraid our gel down here tends to be a bit cold.'

'I don't care if it's like ice, as long as my baby's OK,' she said, and pulled the hem of her top up so he could smear the radio-conductive gel over her abdomen.

He ran the transceiver head over her abdomen and begged silently, oh, please let the baby be kicking away.

The ultrasound didn't show any sign of a blood clot, but it did show him the thing he'd been dreading: the baby wasn't moving and there was no heartbeat.

Oh, hell. He was going to have to deliver the worst possible news. This was the bit of his job he really, really hated.

Theo arrived just before Harry could open his mouth. 'You asked to see me, Dr Gardiner?'

'Yes. Thank you for coming. Excuse me a second,' Harry said to Mrs Freeman. 'I just want to have a quick word with Mr Petrakis, our senior obstetric consultant. I'll introduce you properly in a moment.'

He walked away and said to Theo in a low voice, 'I couldn't pick up the fetal heartbeat. I know that's common in the first trimester, but also there's no movement or heartbeat showing on the ultrasound. The mum's not bleeding and I couldn't see a clot, and there's no sign right at this moment of hypovolaemic shock—but, given that it was blunt trauma and what's happened to the fetus, I think we're looking at a concealed placental abruption.'

'Sounds like it,' Theo said. 'Poor woman. In that case we need to restore her blood volume before she goes into shock and we'll have to deliver the baby PV—it's the only way to stop the bleeding from the abruption. And I'll want to admit her to the ward for monitoring in case she goes into DIC.'

Harry went back over to Mrs Freeman with Theo and introduced the specialist to her. Theo looked at the ultrasound and from the expression in the consultant's eyes Harry could tell that his original diagnosis was indeed correct. They wouldn't have time to wait for her husband to arrive to break the news; they needed to treat her now, before she went into shock.

He sat down beside her on the opposite side from Isla and held her other hand. 'Mrs Freeman, I'm so sorry. There is no nice way to tell you this, but I'm afraid the accident caused what we call a placental abruption. Basically it means that the force of the accident made your placenta detach from the uterus.'

'What about my baby?'

'I'm so sorry,' he said. 'We still need to treat you, but I'm afraid there's nothing we can do for the baby.'

She stared at him in horror. 'My baby's dead?' she whispered.

'I'm so sorry,' he said again. If only he could make this right. But there was nothing that anyone could do.

Mrs Freeman was shaking. Fat tears were rolling down her cheeks, but she made no sound. What he was seeing was total desolation. And it wasn't fixable.

Isla had her arm round Mrs Freeman's shoulders, doing her best to comfort her.

Feeling helpless, Harry explained what they were going to do next and that they needed to keep her in for a little while to keep an eye on her.

Halfway through treatment her husband arrived and Harry had to break the bad news all over again.

'I'm so sorry, Mr Freeman,' he finished.

Mr Freeman looked dazed. 'Our baby's dead? And Paulette?'

'We're treating her now, but we want to keep her in for monitoring. Would you like to come and be with her?'

'Yes—I— Is she going to be all right?'

'She's going to be fine,' Harry reassured him. 'I'm just so sorry I can't give you better news.'

By the time Harry's shift finished, he was completely drained. The last thing he felt like doing was talking to Isla to find out what was wrong, but he knew it had to be done. Maybe he could arrange to see her tomorrow and they could sort it out then. When they'd both had time to recover from their rough day.

But when he saw her outside the staff kitchen, he could see that she'd been crying.

'Are you all right?' he asked softly, even though he knew it was a stupid question; it was obvious that she wasn't OK at all.

'Rough shift,' she said. 'You should know. You were there.'

'Yeah.' He closed his eyes for a moment. 'I hate breaking that kind of news to people. I hate seeing their dreams shatter like that.' He opened his eyes again. 'I don't know about you, but I can't face going anywhere and talking tonight. Shall we just get a pizza and go back to my place?'

'I…' She dragged in a breath. 'Harry, we really need to talk.'

He went cold. The way she was talking sounded horribly final. Just like the way he'd always broken the news to whoever he was dating that it wasn't really working and he'd rather they just stayed as friends.

Was Isla going to end it between them?

But surely not right now—not after the day they'd both had.

Not feeling up to talking, he asked, 'Can this wait until tomorrow?'

She shook her head. 'It's already been dragging on too long.'

He really didn't like the sound of that. He had a nasty feeling that he knew why she'd been distant, these last few days: because she was ending it.

'Is that café round the corner still open?' she asked.

He guessed that she meant the one where he'd taken her for a bacon sandwich, the morning after the night shift where the drunk had come on to her. 'We can take a look,' he said. 'Is that where you want to go?'

'It'll be a lot more private than the hospital canteen. It means we can talk.'

'OK.'

They walked to the café in silence. Harry could feel himself getting more and more tense, the nearer they got to the café; and, even though he was trying to prepare himself for being dumped, it just hurt too damn much. He didn't want it to end between them. He wanted to take it forward. Take the risk.

'Tea and a bacon sandwich?' he asked outside the door to the café.

She shook her head. 'Just a glass of water for me, thanks.'

'OK. If you find us a table, I'll sort out the drinks.' He ordered himself a mug of tea, to put off the moment that little bit longer.

When the waitress sorted out the drinks, Harry discovered that Isla had found them a quiet table out of the way. Good.

Well, he wasn't going to be weak and wait to be dumped. He was going to initiate the discussion and ask up front. 'So are you going to tell me what I've done wrong?' he asked as he sat down.

'Wrong? What do you mean, wrong?'

'It feels as if you've been avoiding me for the last few days,' he said. And he was aware how ironic it was that they'd had this conversation before—except, last time, he'd been the one doing the avoiding.

'That's because I have,' she said softly.

Pain lanced through him. He hadn't been imagining it, then. She was going to end it—and she'd been working out how to tell him, the last few days. While he, being a fool, had been thinking about moving their relationship on to the next step.

'So what did I do wrong?' he repeated.

'Nothing.'

He didn't get it. 'So why were you avoiding me?'

She took a deep breath. 'There isn't an easy way to say this.'

So she was definitely ending it—and he was shocked to realise how much it hurt. How much she meant to him and how empty his life was going to be without her.

This was one of the hardest things Isla had ever done. She hated the fact that her words were going to blow Harry's world apart. She was just about to make his worst nightmare come true.

But he'd clearly already worked out that something wasn't right.

Even though her timing wasn't brilliant—he

was already feeling low after a rotten shift—she couldn't keep it from him any longer.

'I'm pregnant,' she said.

He looked at her, saying absolutely nothing—and she couldn't tell a thing from his expression. How he was feeling, what he was thinking… nothing.

'With our baby,' she clarified. Not that there could be any mistake. They'd both been faithful to each other.

Still he said nothing. He just stared at her as if he couldn't believe what he was hearing. He looked shocked to the core.

Well, what had she expected? That he'd throw his arms round her and tell her how thrilled he was?

He'd made it clear enough that he never wanted children, and she was telling him that he was going to be a father—exactly what he didn't want.

The fact that he'd said nothing at all made it very obvious that he hadn't changed his mind. He just didn't know how to tell her without hurting her.

So she was going to have to be brave and be the one to walk away.

'It's all right,' she said, even though it wasn't and it left her feeling bone-deep tired and unutterably sad. 'I know you don't want children. I'm not expecting anything from you, and I understand that it's the end between us.'

And it was clear what she needed to do next. This was Harry's patch. He'd lived in London since he was a student; he'd trained and worked in the same hospital for twelve years. She'd been in the emergency department at the London Victoria for only a few months. It was obvious which of the two of them would have to leave.

'I'm going home to Scotland,' she said. 'To the island. But I didn't want to leave without telling you why. I'm sorry, Harry.'

And she got up to leave.

CHAPTER THIRTEEN

SHOCK RADIATED THROUGH HARRY.

He couldn't believe what he was hearing.

Isla was pregnant?

With his baby?

Well, of *course* his baby—she wasn't the sort to have an affair. He knew that without having to ask.

But he couldn't quite process the idea of being a father. He couldn't say a word. It felt as if his mouth had been filled with glue. And someone had glued him to his seat, too, because Isla was walking away from him and he was still stuck here, watching her leave.

This had to be a nightmare. One of those hyper-real dreams where the situation was so close to real life that it could really be happening, but there was something out of kilter that would tell you it was all a figment of your imagination.

Like being stuck to your seat. Like there being no sound at all, even though they were in a café and there would usually be the hiss of steam from a coffee machine and the sound of a spoon clinking against a mug as sugar was stirred in, the low buzz of other people talking.

He'd wake up in a second. It'd be stupid o'clock in the morning, and he'd be in either his own bed or Isla's, spooned round her body. He'd hear her soft, regular breathing and he'd know that this was just a dream and all was right with the world.

Any second now.

Any second now.

But then the door closed behind her and the sound all seemed to rush back in—like the moment when a tube train arrived at the station, and all the noise echoed everywhere. Hissing steam, clinking spoons and mugs, the hum of conversation.

Oh, dear God.

This wasn't a nightmare.

Isla was pregnant, she was planning to leave London, and…

No, no, no.

He couldn't let her leave.

He needed to talk to her. Tell her how he felt about her. Ask her to stay. Beg her to stay. On his knees, if he had to.

He could do with someone tipping a bucket of ice-cold water over him to shock his brain back into working again, so he could find the right words to ask her to stay. Failing that, he'd just have to hope that he could muddle his way through it.

Ignoring the startled looks of the other customers in the café, he left his unfinished mug of tea where it was and rushed out after Isla.

He looked out either side of the door in the street. He thought he caught sight of her walking away and called out, 'Isla, wait!'

Either she hadn't heard him or the woman wasn't actually Isla. Inwardly praying that it was the former, he ran after her and finally caught up with her.

Thank God. It was her.

'Isla, wait,' he said again.

She stopped and stared at him. 'Why? You

made it perfectly clear just now that you didn't want to know.'

'Did I, hell.'

'I told you the news and you didn't say a word.'

'You didn't exactly give me a chance!' he protested.

'I did,' she said. 'I sat there like a lemon, staring at you and waiting for you to say something.'

'I was too shocked to think straight, let alone for my mouth to work. I needed a few seconds for the news to sink in. And now it has. I think.'

She blinked back the tears. 'Harry, you've told me often enough that you don't want kids and you don't want to settle down. I'm not expecting you to change for me.'

'What if I want to change?' he asked.

She shook her head. 'I can't ask you to do that.'

'You're not asking me. I'm offering.'

'No. Don't make any sacrifices, because you'll regret it later. Anything you decide has to be because you really, really want it. You can't live your life to please other people.'

'I don't want you to leave,' he said. 'Stay.'

'If I go home to Scotland, at least I'll have my

family round me to help with the baby. If I stay here, I'll be struggling on my own,' she pointed out. 'It makes sense to leave.'

'So you want to keep the baby?'

She dragged in a breath. 'You can actually ask me that after what happened at work today, when that poor woman lost a baby she clearly wanted very much?'

He winced. 'Sorry, that came out wrong. I don't mean that at all. Just—we didn't plan this, did we? Either of us. We haven't talked properly about what we want out of life. We've been taking this thing between us one step at a time.' He dragged a hand through his hair. 'I'm making a mess of this, but we need to talk about it, and I can't let you just walk away from me—and the street really isn't the right place to discuss this. Your place or mine?'

'I guess yours is nearer,' she said.

'Mine it is, then—and there's no pressure. We'll just talk things through, and then, if you want me to drive you back to yours afterwards, I will.' He blew out a breath. 'Just talk to me, Isla. You once said to me that you weren't a mind-reader.

Neither am I. And I really need to know what's going on in your head.'

She looked at him, and for a nasty moment he thought she was going to refuse; but then she nodded.

They walked back to his place in uneasy silence. He tried letting his hand accidentally brush against hers, but she didn't let her fingers curl round his, so he gave up. Maybe she was right. Maybe they needed to do this with a clear head, not let the attraction between them get in the way and muddle things up.

'Can I get you a drink?' he asked once they were in his living room.

'No, thanks.'

Were they really reduced to cool politeness? But then he found himself lapsing into it, too. 'Please, have a seat.'

He noticed that she picked one of the chairs rather than the sofa, making it clear that she didn't want him right next to her. He pushed the hurt aside. OK. He could deal with this. He needed to give her a little bit of space. Clearly she was upset and worried, and all the hormonal changes of pregnancy weren't helping the situation one little bit.

Hoping that she wouldn't misinterpret where he sat, he chose a seat on the sofa opposite her. All he wanted to do was to hold her and tell her that everything was going to be all right. But how could he promise her that, when he didn't know that it would be anywhere near all right?

What a mess.

He didn't even know where to start. Emotionally, this was a total minefield and it was way outside his experience. So he fell back on the thing he knew he was good at. Being a doctor. Maybe that would be the best place to start. 'Are you all right?' he asked. 'I mean, are you having morning sickness or headaches?'

'It's not been brilliant,' she admitted.

'How long have you known?'

She took a deep breath. 'I did the test nearly a week ago.'

So she'd had a week to get used to the idea and work out how she felt about it, whereas he'd only had a few scant minutes—and it wasn't anywhere near enough. 'When you thought you had the bug that was going round?' he asked.

'Except it wasn't that.'

Now he was beginning to understand why she'd backed off from him—because she'd discovered she was pregnant and she'd been scared of his reaction. Because he'd told her often enough that he didn't want kids. He just hadn't told her why. And maybe it was time he explained. 'I'm sorry,' he said. 'You should've been able to tell me. And I feel bad that I'm not approachable enough for you to have said anything before.'

'We didn't exactly plan this, did we?' She bit her lip. 'And we were careful.'

Not careful enough. The only guaranteed form of conception was abstinence. 'Do you know how pregnant you are?'

'The test said more than three weeks. My last period was very light, but I thought...' She shrugged. 'Well, obviously I was wrong.'

'Isla, I don't know what to say,' he admitted. 'I really wasn't expecting this.' He raked a hand through his hair. 'And, after a day like today...'

'I couldn't keep it to myself any longer,' she

said. 'Not after today. Because what happened to that poor woman made me think, what if it had been me? I hadn't really let myself think too much about the baby and what options I had. But after sitting there, holding her hand while you told her the bad news, it became really clear to me what I wanted.'

To keep the baby. She'd already told him that. But what else? Did she want to bring up the baby on her own, or with him?

And what did he want?

He'd had no time to think about it, to weigh up the options. He'd always been so sure that he didn't want children. So very sure. But now he was going to be a dad, and he didn't have a clue what to say.

'I've been trying to work out for the last week how to tell you. I knew it was your worst nightmare,' she said, almost as if she could read his mind. But then she frowned. 'But what I really don't understand, Harry, is why you're so sure you don't want kids. You're so good with them at work—and at the wedding, you were great with little Evan. And when we went away, you were lovely with that little girl on the beach who stood on the weever fish—you told her a story to keep her mind off how much her foot hurt. You'd make such a great father. I don't understand why you'd cut yourself off from all that potential love. Is it because you have so many brothers and sisters, but you didn't grow up with most of them?'

'No.' He blew out a breath. Maybe if he told her the misery that had haunted him for years, she'd get it. 'Do you remember the little boy who'd eaten his grandfather's iron tablets?'

'Yes.' She looked puzzled. 'Why?'

'And you remember I told his grandmother that toddlers were unpredictable?'

'Yes.'

'And I know that's true, because I've walked in her shoes,' he said softly.

She stared at him. 'What, you had a toddler who accidentally ate iron tablets—one who died?'

'Not my toddler and not iron tablets and no death, but something bad happened, something that's haunted me ever since,' he said. 'I was eleven. Mum had just popped out to the shops and she asked me to keep an eye on my sisters.

Maisie was five, Tasha was two, and Bibi was a baby. I thought it'd be all right. I put Maisie and Tasha in front of the telly—there was some cartoon on they both liked—and I was doing my homework at the dining room table. French, I remember. Then Bibi started crying. Maisie came and told me the baby was all stinky, so I knew I had to change her nappy—I couldn't just leave her crying until Mum got home. I thought the others would be fine in front of the telly while I took the baby upstairs and changed her.'

'What happened?' she asked softly.

'I forgot to close the stair gate,' he said. 'Tasha got bored with the telly and decided to come and find me. I had the baby in my arms, and I saw Tasha get to the top of the stairs. She was smiling and so pleased with herself. Then she wobbled and fell backwards. Right down the whole flight of stairs. Before I could get to her. Everything happened in slow motion—I could see it happening, but I couldn't do a thing about it. And then she was just lying there at the bottom of the stairs and she wasn't making a sound. I thought she was dead and it was all my fault.'

'This is your middle sister, yes? And she wasn't...?'

He shook his head. 'She survived.' Though she hadn't made a complete recovery.

'Harry, just about anyone would struggle to look after three children under five, and you were only eleven years old at the time,' Isla pointed out. 'You were doing your best. You were busy changing the baby. You weren't to know that your two-year-old sister would fall down the stairs.'

'I know—but if I'd closed the stair gate it wouldn't have happened.'

'Or she might have gone into the kitchen or the garden and hurt herself there instead,' Isla said. 'You're right about toddlers being unpredictable, and you can't blame yourself—plus it's so easy to see things differently with hindsight. It's not fair to blame yourself. What did your mum say?'

'She came home to find an ambulance outside our house with a flashing blue light,' Harry said, 'so she was pretty shocked—and her first words to me were that she'd trusted me to look after the girls while she went to get some bread and some milk, and why hadn't I kept a proper eye on them?'

Isla winced. 'That to me sounds like a panicky mum who isn't thinking straight.'

'She apologised later,' Harry said. 'She told me that it wasn't my fault.' He paused. 'But we both knew it was, and she never asked me to look after the girls again on my own after that.'

'I bet she was feeling just as guilty—she was the adult, and she'd left you in charge of three young children, when you were still only a child yourself,' Isla pointed out. 'And how far away were the shops?'

'A fifteen-minute walk,' Harry said. 'Not far—but it was long enough for me to nearly kill Tasha. I had bad dreams for months about it. I saw my little sister lying at the bottom of the stairs, her face white, and I couldn't see her breathing. I never wanted to go through fear like that again, and that was when I vowed that I'd never have kids of my own. I didn't want that responsibility—or to let another child down.'

Isla left her seat, came over to him and hugged him fiercely. 'You were a child yourself, Harry, and having that kind of a responsibility as a child is completely different from having it as an adult. And she was fine, wasn't she?'

That was the big question. 'The hospital said it was concussion and a broken arm.' He bit his lip. 'We thought she'd recovered just fine over the next few weeks. But over the months, Mum noticed that Tasha was always off in a dream world. When she got a bit older, if she was reading, you had to take the book out of her hands to get her to realise you'd been calling her.'

'Because she lost herself in the book?'

He shook his head. 'Mum talked to the health visitor about it. They thought she might have glue ear. But when the audiology department at the hospital tested her, they found out that actually, her hearing was damaged permanently.' This was the crunch bit. 'According to the audiogram, what was wrong was impact damage—so it had been caused by the fall. Because I didn't look after her properly, Tasha's on the border of being severely deaf, and for certain pitches she's profoundly deaf—she can't hear really deep voices.'

'Plenty of people cope with deafness,' Isla

pointed out gently, 'and I get the impression from what you've told me about your sisters that they're all very independent.'

'They are,' he admitted. 'But don't you see? Her deafness was caused by the fall. It shouldn't have happened. And I feel bad that she's always had to struggle and work harder than everyone else. She was bright enough to pick things up from books, but half the time she couldn't actually hear what the teachers were saying. Even with hearing aids, it's difficult—when she's in noisy surroundings, it's hard to pick up what people are saying, especially if they have quiet voices or they're in her difficult range and she can't see their faces to lip-read. She has to concentrate so much harder to pick up all the social stuff as well as cope with work.'

'Is that how she sees it?' Isla asked.

'Well—no. We fight about it,' Harry admitted. 'She refuses to be defined by her hearing. She says I'm over-protective and it drives her crazy.'

'Have you tried putting yourself in her shoes?' Isla asked softly.

'Yes. And I still blame myself. And I'll always

remember how I felt, seeing her lying there on the floor, not moving. That choking feeling of panic.' He dragged in a breath. 'I see parents most weeks who are panicking as much as I did back then. Parents who are worried sick about a baby or a toddler with a virus or a severe allergic reaction. I think the fear's the same, however old or however experienced you are.' He paused. 'And I guess that's part of why I didn't want to get involved with anyone. I didn't want to risk things going wrong. I told myself that getting involved with someone, getting married and having kids…that wasn't for me.'

Isla swallowed hard. 'And then I came along.'

'And you changed everything,' he said. 'You made me see that things might be different to what I always thought they were. That, just because my parents had made mistakes, it didn't mean that I was necessarily going to repeat them.' He took a deep breath. 'So if I was wrong about that, maybe I'm wrong about other things, too. Like not wanting children.'

'So what are you saying?'

'I'm saying,' he said, 'that I need a little time to

let it sink in and to come to terms with it. Right now, I'm still shocked and I feel as if someone's smacked me over the head with a frying pan. But give me a little time to think about it and get used to the idea. You've had a week, and I've only had a few minutes. I can't adjust that fast, Isla, no matter how much I want to. I'm only human.'

'I'm sorry. I'm being selfish.' Her eyes misted with tears.

She looked as if she was going to pull away from him, but he wrapped his arms round her and hauled her onto his lap. 'Isla. These last couple of weeks, I've been doing a lot of thinking myself. And this week I thought that you were avoiding me because you were working out how to dump me—'

'Dump you?' she interrupted.

'Dump me,' he repeated. 'I'd been thinking about us. About how I like being with you. About how my world's a better place when I wake up in your arms in the morning. About how you make me want to be brave and take the risk of a real grown-up relationship.' He paused. 'I had been thinking about asking you to move in with me.'

He paused again. 'This is probably too little, too late. But I'm going to tell you anyway, because you can't read what I'm thinking. I was going to ask you to get engaged.' He swallowed hard. 'To take the really big risk and get married.'

'What? *You* want to get married?' She looked at him in utter shock.

'Yes.' He gave her a wry smile. 'I didn't believe it either, at first. But the thing is, I met someone. Someone I really like. Someone I really believe in and who seems to believe in me, too. Someone who told me that I was capable of really loving someone. She made me think about it properly for the first time ever.' He paused. 'And you were right. I am capable of loving someone. I love you, Isla McKenna. And, if you'll have me, I'd very much like to marry you.'

'Uh…' She stared at him. 'I think it's my turn to have the frying pan moment. Did you just ask me to marry you?'

'I did.'

'Me *and* our baby?' she checked.

'I believe you come as a package,' he said dryly.

'But—you—me—how?' she asked plaintively.

He stroked her face. 'Now I definitely know you're pregnant. The hormones have put a gag on all that strident Scottish common sense.'

'Have they, hell. Harry, you're allergic to marriage.'

'There's no immunoglobulin reaction, as far as I can tell,' he said, starting to relax and enjoy himself.

'You said you didn't want to settle down. Ever.'

'Tsk—are you so old-fashioned that you think it's only a woman's prerogative to change her mind?'

'Harry Gardiner, you're the most impossible—'

He judged that he'd teased her enough. So he stopped her words by the simple act of kissing her. 'I love you, Isla,' he said when he broke the kiss. 'I might even have loved you from the first day I met you. But every day I've worked with you, or dated you, or woken with you in my arms, I've got to know you a little more and I've grown to love you a little more. And although I admit I'm absolutely terrified at the idea of being a dad—and I'm even more terrified by the idea that I might let our child down, the way I let my sister down—I know I'm going to make it work because you'll be at my side. And, with you by my side, I know I can do absolutely anything. Because I can talk to you, and you can make me see sense. And you can talk to me, knowing I'll always back you and take your part. We're a team, Isla. Not just at work.'

A tear spilled over and trickled down her cheek, and he kissed it away.

'Hormones,' she said.

He coughed. 'Wrong word. The one you're looking for has one syllable, three letters, and starts with the twenty-fifth letter of the alphabet. The middle letter's a vowel. And the last letter's often used as a plural. Got it?'

'You didn't actually ask me,' she pointed out. 'You said, if I'll have you, you'd like to marry me. Which isn't the same as asking me.'

'Yes, it is.'

She just looked at him.

He sighed, shifted her off his lap, and got down on one knee before her. 'If you're being picky about it, I also don't have a ring—and am I not supposed to present you with a ring if I do it the traditional way?'

'You said you'll back me. That's enough.' She flapped a dismissive hand. 'We don't need flashy gemstones.'

He laughed. 'Ah, the Scottish tartness is reasserting itself. Good. Isla McKenna, I love you. And I'm still terrified out of my wits about being a dad, but I know I'll love our baby just as much as I love you. Will you marry me?'

She smiled. 'Yes.'

He coughed.

'What?' she asked.

'You haven't said it,' he reminded her. 'Three little words. And I've spent the last week in a bad place, thinking that you were going to walk out on me. I need a little TLC.'

'Ah, the three little words. Tender, loving care.'

'Three *smaller* words,' he said, giving her a pained look. 'Come on. I said it first.'

'I know. And I'm glad.' She smiled. 'I love you, too, Harry Gardiner. I think I did from the second you kissed me in the moonlight in Cornwall. And I admit that I, too, am just a little bit panicky about whether I'm going to be a good enough mum. But with you by my side, I think the answer's going to be yes. It's like you said. We're a team. Things might not always go smoothly, but we'll always have each other's back.'

'You'd better believe it,' he said softly.

EPILOGUE

Three months later

'WE SHOULD'VE ELOPED,' Harry said. 'How about I go and borrow a horse and a tricorn hat, kidnap you and carry you off to my lair?'

Isla laughed. 'Are the boys giving you a hard time?'

'Not just the boys. Five best men. *Five.* It's excessive. And then the girls accused me of sexism and demanded to know why they couldn't be best women. All of them.' He groaned. 'I can't possibly have eight best men and women on my wedding day!'

'As you're only going to get married once, none of them wants to miss out, so I don't think you have much choice,' Isla said. 'And I'm surprised your father hasn't tried to make it nine.'

'He did. He said I'd been his best man so I ought

to let him be one of mine. I reminded him that he's already got a role as the father of the groom,' Harry said. 'But the others… They're supposed to let the oldest sibling boss them around, not the other way round. They're impossible!'

Isla laughed again, knowing that his grumbling was more for show than anything else. Since Harry had opened his heart to her, he'd also opened his heart to his brothers and sisters—and as a result he'd become much, much closer to his whole family. 'I love your brothers and sisters. They're so like you. Totally irrepressible.'

He groaned. 'So much for a quiet wedding. We really should've disappeared to Gretna Green.'

'Scotland? Hmm. I don't think that would've been quiet, either. And you do know my family's planning on teaching yours to party the Scots way tonight, don't you?'

'We definitely need to run away,' Harry said.

'I think it's a little too late for that. We're supposed to be in church in two hours. And you're not supposed to be here, much less talking to me through a closed door.'

'You're the one who insisted that it was bad

luck to see me on our wedding day before you got to the church,' he reminded her. 'That's why I'm talking to you through a closed door. Are you quite sure we can't elope?'

'Harry, stop panicking,' she said. 'Go with the flow and let your siblings enjoy your wedding. Because you're only getting married once.'

He sighed. 'Our poor baby doesn't know what he or she has in store.'

'Oh, I think he or she does,' Isla corrected, 'and I think this is going to be the most loved baby in history.'

'And definitely by his—or her—dad.' Harry had been in tears at the scan, and had been a besotted father-to-be ever since.

'See you at church,' she said softly. 'And thank you for the beautiful necklace. It goes perfectly with my dress.'

'Well, you needed a "something new" to wear. It's traditional.' He coughed. 'It's also traditional to give your husband a kiss for a gift.'

'I will. At the altar,' she promised. 'I love you, Harry. And today's going to be fun. Really.'

And it was. Right from the moment Isla walked

up the aisle on her father's arm, seeing the small church absolutely bursting at the seams with all their family and their friends from work, through to seeing the love in Harry's eyes as he turned to face her at the altar, through to everyone throwing dried rose petals over them both as they walked out of the church as man and wife.

The reception was even better. And Isla really enjoyed the best-men-and-women's speeches. Harry's brothers and sisters had clearly got together before the wedding and practised, because they all lined up on the stage behind the top table.

'The best man's speech is supposed to be short,' Evan said, starting them off, 'but we all wanted to be the best man and made Harry let us all do it, and we all want to say something so the speech won't be very short. It's funny, though. And I'm going to tell you a joke. What did the banana say to the monkey?'

The others all chorused, 'Nothing, bananas can't talk!' and did a little tap-dance with jazz hands, making everyone at the reception laugh.

Harry's siblings went in age order after that, with each of them telling a Harry story that made everyone laugh, though Isla noticed that Harry's middle sister seemed to have missed her slot.

But then, when Jack had finished speaking, Tasha took the microphone. 'My Harry story isn't a funny one. But it's about the bravest, best man I know. When I was two, I fell all the way down the stairs and I broke my arm. A few months later, we worked out that the fall had made me deaf in one ear, too. Harry's always blamed himself for what happened, but there's no way he could've rescued me when he was right in the middle of changing Bibi's nappy. We all think he's a superhero, but even he can't be in two places at once.'

Isla slipped her hand into Harry's, and squeezed his fingers.

'Without him, I wouldn't be a trainee audiologist, and I wouldn't be able to understand my patients as well as I do,' Tasha continued. 'And actually, I'm kind of glad it happened, because I know it was one of the reasons why he became a doctor—and the emergency department of the London Victoria wouldn't be the same without him.'

There were loud cheers of agreement from Harry and Isla's colleagues.

'And because he's an emergency doctor, that meant that he met Isla at work. We're all so glad he did, because she's the best thing to happen to him, and it's lovely to see my big brother get the happiness he never thought he deserved—but he really *does* deserve it.' She lifted her glass. 'So the best men and women all want you to raise your glasses now for a toast—to Harry and Isla, and may their life together be full of happiness.'

Harry stole a kiss from Isla as everyone chorused the toast. 'Yes. It's never going to be quiet, but it's going to be full of happiness,' he said with a smile. 'I love you. And our baby. And our chaotic, wonderful extended family.'

'Me, too.' Isla smiled back. 'I'm with you all the way. Always.'

* * * * *

MILLS & BOON®
Large Print Medical

August

His Shock Valentine's Proposal	Amy Ruttan
Craving Her Ex-Army Doc	Amy Ruttan
The Man She Could Never Forget	Meredith Webber
The Nurse Who Stole His Heart	Alison Roberts
Her Holiday Miracle	Joanna Neil
Discovering Dr Riley	Annie Claydon

September

The Socialite's Secret	Carol Marinelli
London's Most Eligible Doctor	Annie O'Neil
Saving Maddie's Baby	Marion Lennox
A Sheikh to Capture Her Heart	Meredith Webber
Breaking All Their Rules	Sue MacKay
One Life-Changing Night	Louisa Heaton

October

Seduced by the Heart Surgeon	Carol Marinelli
Falling for the Single Dad	Emily Forbes
The Fling That Changed Everything	Alison Roberts
A Child to Open Their Hearts	Marion Lennox
The Greek Doctor's Secret Son	Jennifer Taylor
Caught in a Storm of Passion	Lucy Ryder

MILLS & BOON®
Large Print Medical

November

December

January